A Québécois Dream

VICTOR-LÉVY BEAULIEU

A QUÉBÉCOIS DREAM

TRANSLATED BY RAY CHAMBERLAIN

Exile Editions, Toronto

This edition is published by Exile Editions Limited, 20 Dale Avenue, Toronto, Canada. Both the translator and the publisher wish to acknowledge the Canada Council and the Ontario Arts Council for financial assistance towards publication.

Exile Editions are distributed in Canada and the United States by Firefly Books, 2 Essex Avenue, Unit #5, Thornhill, Ontario.

Designed by Tim Inkster, typeset in Garamond by The Coach House Press (Toronto), printed and bound by the Porcupine's Quill, Inc. (Erin) in December of 1978. The stock is Zephyr Antique Laid.

ISBN 0-920428-18-5

To Madame Rosa Rose,
Very Respectfully

I make my plans
with the dreams of my sleeping soldiers –

(Jeanne D'Arc)

offend me
that I might have the strength to kill you –

(Paul Valéry)

CUT ONE

((It happened when he stepped onto des Récollets Street: he could tell something was different all of a sudden. A cloud hovering over him like a dusky wing and right away this feeling of oppression. His legs were hurting. Goddamn creaky knees! He lifted a foot and set it down slowly. He took off his cap. His curly, matted hair. Damn sweat! He wiped his forehead. If at least I had a car. He saw himself at the wheel of an old convertible tearing through the streets of Morial Mort. He'd put on seat covers to hide the rips and the cigarette burns in the worn leather. The tires squealed on the asphalt; he'd slam on the brakes at red lights, and the Hollywood mufflers made a hell of a racket when he took off again. The fox tail fixed on the antenna was an occult trophy, some strange symbol of virility. He had the radio turned up all the way: it was blaring, really blasting out of the back speaker. Think I don't know how to handle cunt, mother-fucker! And there sure are some out on the prowl this mornin'! Truth was, there were lots of them − girls on the street in summer outfits − You know, the kind of clothes that show everything without showing anything, those scanty things that show off the navel and the place where mongoloids are made. Hey, get a load of those big, high-class asses in those shorts! He must have been walking for an hour now, long strides beneath a leaden sun. The arm holding the overnight bag'd gone to sleep a long time ago. Even his bad leg was growing numb. Good thing there were plenty of taverns along the way for old Joseph-David-Barthélémy Dupuis! He yawned the time to let the novelist see his nicotine-stained

7

teeth and that tongue he could wag as fast as a nervous foot –
and wasn't it wearing a sock right now! It was the beer, it had
knocked him out: KO, CHA-O ...s. But Joseph-David-
Barthélémy Dupuis didn't give a damn! The house wasn't far,
and soon, sucking his Jeanne D'Arc's tits, his barometer'd
show fair weather again. Yeah, sure, he was out of work – so
what? There're more than enough people workin' already!
He hawked up phlegm and spit it out on the sidewalk, then
cleared his throat. Somethin' stunk. Too many women on the
rag, most likely. He figured Jeanne D'Arc was parked naked
in front of the television set watching some crummy film,
holding her heavy, brown tits in her hands. His hand tightened into a fist; he couldn't help it: I don't trust her, an' I got
good reasons not to. Hers ain't the most Catholic cunt in the
world, the lousy bitch! He might have added that he didn't
do much to help her there, and that he wasn't exactly a model
husband. But what would be the point? Everybody in Morial
Mort knew that, starting with his Jeanne D'Arc. (You're a
no-good bum, understand? That's what bugs me!) He would
pinch one of her tits, laughing a manly laugh. Usually it
worked: all he had to do was tickle a tit and she'd calm down.
But this mornin' it didn't do any good: she slapped shit outta
me and me too stupid to slap her back. I took my cap off the
nail an' – ahhh! What he had done was simple enough: he had
slammed the door, slammed it so hard a pane of glass tumbled out onto the floor and broke all to pieces. And Jeanne
D'Arc screaming when he jumped over the fence – Bastard!
You're nothing but a coward, a drunken bum! He'd shrugged
his shoulders. Women always scream the same thing. First of
all, I'm not a drunk. I have a small Labatt's every now and
then but you gotta wet your whistle when it's hot like this,
eh? He laughed. He liked being a holy terror with his Jeanne
D'Arc. Get fed up? Her? Come on! Was anybody gonna
hump her any better than him in his old parents' big bed?
Yeah, well, that's what worries me: Jeanne D'Arc's got fuckin' on the brain an' maybe she says, another prick that'll keep

8

the juices flowin'. He saw her stretched out in the middle of the old parents' big bed, her legs spread for Christie to feed her one mean sandwich. He chased the thought away in a hurry — Till I'm shown different my Jeanne D'Arc eats the same kind of sandwiches as everybody else. Joseph-David-Barthélémy Dupuis was thinking too much and had hardly noticed things as he passed them, so he was astonished to discover he was almost home. The house's gable was a white maw in the green surroundings. He had just trimmed the trees, whose branches were beating against the upstairs window and keeping Jeanne D'Arc from sleeping. I worked a lot this summer. Yes, he had. He had butchered the hedge of spirea in front of the porch trying to fashion green figures and a cross. Yeah, well, I was bound to mess it up, I got no experience with that sort of thing — I ruined the fuckin' hedge, if you wanna know! He had even hoed up the pumpkins his Jeanne D'Arc was growing by the fence in the back yard. She must really like those big, green balls warmin' their bellies in the sun! Damn if the little woman ain't vulgar! It comes from watchin' TV with all those programs full of nothin' but sex! He laughed again. He laughed a lot lately. Laughter would simply bubble up in his body like witches' brew in a cauldron. He was beginning to enjoy it. He was perfecting his laugh, thickening it and rounding it out. Because soon he was going to undertake something noble; he didn't know what yet, but he was sure he would go down in history. I'm gonna have my fine car an' then my Jeanne D'Arc's gonna be in trouble, then she's gonna get it, but good. Now des Récollets Street had changed while he was gone. What was it all about? You're too tired, probably from walkin' and drinkin' too much. Is it because you just got outta Dorémi, old Joseph-David-Barthélémy Dupuis? An' you're gonna go home and hug and squeeze your Jeanne D'Arc? He didn't really believe it, there was too much noise on des Récollets, too many helicopters circling around and landing somewhere behind the houses in huge clouds of dust

9

with their long, sweeping propellers, too many police sirens and red bubblegum machines on top of the patrol cars, too many soldiers with long carbines on their shoulders. And des Récollets Street closed off by a wall of cops. Joseph-David-Barthélémy Dupuis stopped. His heart. Out of breath. Hey, what's goin' on? For a second he thought it was him they were after, they were going to haul him in because his Jeanne D'Arc had reported him. He punched his cap. It was that hypocrite Jeanne D'Arc's face he was pounding. She sold me out, crossed me. Now what's gonna become of you? He moved forward a bit; he had to go past the police if he wanted to get home. The street was full of people. Big, greasy faces, wide mouth-faces belching out left and right: Can't get through! Can't get through! Turn around! People were crowded together on the hill in the direction of Monselet. They were afraid of the rifles and of the motorcycles coming from every direction. Barthélémy thought of big, buzzing flies, black and wingless. A chill ran up and down him – Those bastards crammed me full of dope. A hand landed on his shoulder. He turned around. You were told to move back. Don't you see you can't get through? He jumped out of the way of a motorcycle. The white cop helmets were golf balls with red eyes and ears. Barthélémy started to run. What is this? The end of the world, or a war, or what? He jostled men and women alike because he wanted to get away as fast as possible from that swelling, threatening sea. On the bare shoulders of sun-blackened men, children were crying. (Could he really know there was no time left to recreate the world, to ring the past around with a heavy palisade of pious folk, a fort of sorts, to protect it against sly, slinking procedure and savage words flying at the skull with tomahawk fury? There was to be no future for him, perhaps; not even a present; for he was already condemned to what had never been, to what would never be, living out his life in dank obscurity, in a rubber snake world coiling and uncoiling around him, motion almost mechanical, banal, the randomness of mere process, the dumbness of a thing overflowing, emptiness' pure lack which sucked at his spine, leaving him only his purposeless wanderings through Morial Mort — to make sense if he could out of the phoney world of Steinberg supermarkets, Laura Secord shops, Smoker's Corners, snack bars, alleyways, cars parked in no-parking zones, houses jammed up against one another to find warmth, making sure nothing and no one holed up in those decorated wombs should ever be lonely or sick or without a telephone to call the doctor when he was ready to die. Did God alone know that the future was to be found cowering in the narrow folds of the steadily shrinking present?) Oh, push open the tavern door so that darkness might take him and bind his hands behind his back and lead him below and leave him for dead. (God almighty. Oh, God almighty!) Barthélémy's ears were still ringing with the sounds of life outside. His eyes were watering. He was an old hound who was going to die far from his bitch, she with life still beating in her. He was the same as he always was when he got out of Dorémi. Which meant he was scared. So he slapped himself hard on the forehead several times, trying to get hold of himself. But he was far gone already, water was cascading now somewhere behind his eyes and only the traditional invocations could do anything for him — Jesus fuckin' Christ! You becomin' afraid of your own shadow? Damn ugly bitch! Jeanne D'Arc's not gonna eat you. Just because you slugged her doesn't mean you oughta have the shakes. Take it easy, old buddy, take it easy! But he couldn't help himself, his teeth were chattering and hot tears fell from his eyes. He had these attacks more and more often and he was powerless against them. He was definitely going to die. He was definitely through. He kicked a table leg. His wrists came free at once. He downed his beer, stood up, then took off running between the tables and through the opening the door suddenly offered. Outside it seemed to him he was a big, unruly horse hightailing it down the street. (Whoa, whoaaa boy!) He pulled on the reins and the taps on his boot

soles sent up sparks off the asphalt. You wanna break your leg
and get sent to the glue factory? He laughed once again. He
never thought he could be so crazy. To celebrate, he took an
old harmonica out of his pocket and began to play, to the
delight of the passers-by, Jeanne D'Arc's favorite reel, the one
she asked for when she was happy and in love with him.
She'd rub up against me and take hold of my prick. Or keep
time with her foot. With the very first notes he shivered
violently. And those bastards at Dorémi, they hid my harp —
he blew hard into his mouth organ and danced on the
sidewalk, happy, so incredibly happy. But Jeanne D'Arc's
waitin' for me, I gotta hurry. (Maybe she'd put perfume
between her legs and in her ears. Am I ever gonna go at that
with my tongue!) But he wasn't getting anywhere, his house
was like a target seen through field glasses: if he went another
five hundred feet he wouldn't be able to turn back, he'd have
to open fire. (All this was taking place at the hour when the
wild animals go down to drink in the Rivière des Prairies. All
this was taking place at the hour when the mighty males stand
watch, backside to backside, while the females contemplate
their antlers in the still water.) Barthélémy's lungs were spitting flames. The old harmonica had turned red in his hands.
His fingers were twisted with pain, his charred nails were
bloody spots. Barthélémy threw the harmonica on the
ground and stomped it furiously. His lips were bleeding, the
eyes in his face, he knew, were burning embers. (I hate your
guts. God, do I hate your guts!) Once the instrument was
demolished he fell to his knees and saw the poor, squashed
thing crawling along the sidewalk. He was full of remorse
then, and of fierce anger against Jeanne D'Arc, who must
have been waiting for him, secure behind the living room
curtains. (It was no longer at watering time that this was
taking place now, but at the silent hour, the hour of inner
lamentation and of the sun closing its red eye behind the
houses along Monselet Street. Barthélémy carefully picked
up what had been his harmonica, looked at it tenderly, kiss-

ing it before putting it in his pocket next to his heart – I'm losin' my grip. I gotta get to the house before I can't find my way at all! He started walking fast, straight ahead. It was like being in a train: the coach window was distorting the lines of the houses. At least doors were opening to let him through. They know I'm in a hurry an' Jeanne D'Arc's pining for me. He'd never liked houses as much as now. He stammered out his thanks, raising his hand high, two fingers forming the ritualistic v. He was beside himself with joy. For the moment, he had to forget Dorémi, his internment, the judge's threats, Jeanne D'Arc's false witness, the night in the cell, the cops' brutality, the drugs injected into his thigh, and a lot of other shit that would come back one of these days and occupy his heart. Finally, here I am! When he reached the gate his legs were shaking. He was exhausted, as though all his energy had seeped out of the wound in his foot. He waited a while so he could catch his breath. He held on to the fence. Didn't somebody have him by the legs trying to drag him away? Weren't the devils gripping his ankles, warning him how important it was not to move an inch? He punched at thin air, then lifted the gate latch. He began to mutter to himself. A sort of song came out of his mouth, one that he must have heard on the radio, though he didn't remember the real words. He was walking now; the sound of his voice had calmed him. He was approaching the house, his paradise regained after all too much suffering. He pictured to himself Jeanne D'Arc's beautiful face as she let him caress her at the head of the stairs, her eyes glassy, her body not moving, her thoughts elsewhere, in a beery coolness, or perhaps nowhere at all, floating peacefully in darkness, an evil demon pacified by his patient aloofness. The stairs creaked under his feet. The sweat. His large checkered handkerchief was soaking wet. He had dropped his bag to stop the muscles in his arm from twitching. He breathed deeply and walked to the other end of the porch looking at the stars, his nostrils open wide to the familiar odors they'd deprived him of for too long. Then,

13

coming back to the door he stumbled over something and fell. He lay silent. He hoped Jeanne D'Arc hadn't heard him fall – I open the door, she doesn't know I'm there an' lookin' at her, she's got a finger in her mouth, is she ever nervous, that Jeanne D'Arc, it must be because of TV, she must think she's in the movies but she's pretty, I can't wait to put my hand on her head. (He was standing up now.) Wanna tell me what it was I tripped over, for God's sake? He reached for whatever it was that had toppled him and ran his hands over it, astonished to discover it was his old overnight bag. It's not hard to recognize it, it's missin' a handle. Jeanne D'Arc must've filled it full of bricks it's so heavy. He unzipped it and plunged both hands inside. At Dorémi I hid under the bed so I could fool around in the bag without bein' bothered. Sonsabitches, they'd want to stick me while I was asleep an' the next day there I was with my mouth hangin' open. I'd keep noddin' out all day an' I couldn't even talk 'cause my jaws wouldn't move. An' they thought I'd take it without sayin' a word. OK, I ate damn good, I'd've been fat as a pig in no time, but those pills, oh no, well, they weren't gonna get me with that. Hee-hee-hee. I fixed 'em when I began to take 'em with coke. Like walkin' into a stone wall; I'd go off my damn nut, I might've killed everyone of 'em; I was highflyin'. Hee-hee-hee-hee. Joseph-David-Barthélémy Dupuis began to empty his bag. Ah, Jeanne D'Arc put everything I own in there. He might have added: including my memory, but he didn't know the word, that is, what he was in the process of doing, laying out his personal effects, the various pieces of his past that he was anxiously, frantically, dragging to the surface – it left him feeling so unreal that he forgot Jeanne D'Arc. The bag. A catch-all. That is, a trap. And he could never reach the end, there were too many things he considered irretrievably lost, sunk, crushed, undone under barrels and barrels of small Labatt's. Suddenly coming face to face with all this terrified him and made him almost delirious. Breath – Hey, have I ever been around! Damn, have I ever been through it or not! He looked at the westclox hands, the phosphorescent numbers. He put it to his ear and shook it because he didn't hear the tick-tock. Not surprisin' it ain't runnin' it's been so long since it was wound. He had completely forgotten he was supposed to go inside and take Jeanne D'Arc in his arms. He wound the clock and listened to the noise the springs made. I'd have really liked to work in a clock factory! Of everything from his past it was the old westclox he liked most, the old dented and rusted body which was just like him, you couldn't wear it out, its stubbornness kept you from ever really getting at it. It was the world he was holding against his ear, his whole existence he held on to so tightly. The metal's hardness. The cracked glass he had never replaced because dust couldn't hurt those rock-solid works. He set the clock down on the chair beside him and stayed a long time watching the progression of its hands. It was to remember, that was why he was doing it. As a form of homage too, no doubt. Because the clock had saved his life lots of times. Too often when he was completely drunk he just couldn't stand it any more: he would see hordes of demons, monsters would leap at his face trying to disfigure him. He didn't know how to talk about those things, there were no words for what he saw, he'd have had to draw a picture. (But the big hippopotamus had reached the foot of the bed: it was breathing ferociously and soon was going to jump on him and crush him beneath its weight.) Hey, Jeanne D'Arc! Hey, damn it! He leapt to his feet. The evil spell had turned into a whirlwind, lifting dust, dead leaves and scraps of paper in the yard. It's time for me to go in an' take Jeanne D'Arc in my arms an' talk to her once and for all. I got so much to tell her, it's been three months now that I been keepin' it all inside me. A blown up balloon full of words, a long series of sentences which would flow from him the minute he opened his mouth lying at Jeanne D'Arc's side in his old parents' big bed after they'd had a good fuck. He'd be delivered from all that was afflicting him, he'd be soft and humble like in those easy, early days. Oh, the little house. The scratching of a clothes line. High banks of snow. An ass like an offering for the eye. Where and when, all of that? In what dream? Before which decisive swig of beer that had destroyed everything? He coughed softly so as not to alert Jeanne D'Arc, then he tried the door. (Locked, damn it.) He fumbled in his pockets but found nothing he could use to force the lock. He thought of the bag; he knelt down and unzipped it. There's gotta be an old piece of wire in here somewhere. His hands burrowed into his life's debris. (Casting aside the dice, the thin chains, the worn-out shoe, the medallions, the handkerchiefs, the false nose and fake eyeglasses, the doll's head, its eyes hanging out of its sockets, finally coming up with this narrow metal rod with small plastic wheels at both ends which still turned.) Barthélémy unscrewed the wheels and tossed them in the bag. The kodak. The muffled noise (Jeanne D'Arc peeking out from behind the window?) He slid the metal pin into the lock. Easy, easy, don't scare away the birds that've built their nest in there. The sound of breathing through the nose. (And that big draught-horse stepping sleepily through the potato plants. Whoa boy, don't bolt on me now, damn you!) Joseph-David-Barthélémy Dupuis was nervous, you see. And I got no patience, my nerves ain't so hot these days. He kept at it, slowly working the little truck axle into the lock. The springs (he knew there were no springs but he liked to say that word that sounded so nice, that made him think of motion, something like the wild flight of two terrified beasts down des Récollets) — so the springs, then, gave: there was a sort of click, and when he turned the door knob there it was, the long hallway of paradise regained running straight up to him. He was overjoyed, his head full of scenes of the time before Dorémi, only the nice ones, and leaning with his hand against the white plaster wall he understood how close he'd come to dying and losing his Jeanne D'Arc. (No. A mole no more. No more to roam dark holes. No more to be surrounded by stray dogs, their paws bloodied from scrabbling in ice-encrusted snow. No more. No. He was full of fine resolutions, full of tender words he was finally going to say – to himself as much as to his Jeanne D'Arc.) To keep from speaking yet he closed his mouth and sealed his lips with adhesive tape. It was thus that he wandered through paradise regained, invisible in the shadows, and silent, and terribly troubled by what was welling up inside him, all of it somehow constituting his affection for Jeanne D'Arc. I should have taken a bath before I left. And if I had my suit. And my good polished boots. And my tie with the shiny stickpin. Or if I was naked. You can't tell I'm ugly when it's dark. The scars disappear, an' the sores on my foot, too. I'm presentable then. He was sweating profusely and talking to himself in his head because inside things were churning. One wrong move an' I'm caught. Jeanne D'Arc'll be at me tooth and nail. (The truth was he didn't dare admit he was worried, that a knot of anguish had come to his throat the minute he stepped onto des Récollets Street. At a certain point I'm gonna open a door and then – Jeanne D'Arc.) He saw her naked on the sofa, her neck broken, her head, its long blond hair like a torchlight, hanging over the side, soaked in warm blood, her belly open, the smell of piss and shit. That obsession again! He was trying to calm down; he leaned against the wall and closed his eyes – Sickly, pale infant in a stroller with rusty wheels. Then battles with baseball bats somewhere along the Rivière des Prairies. And big caved-in bellies with pieces of intestine sticking out like mushrooms. And quick kisses through the bars to make of love something poor and difficult, to make it nothing but two obscene tongues trying to meet. And happiness right at hand when once alone in the huge, white room at Dorémi. (You're a little boy. Everything's big. Steinberg's parking lot is a black sea. You go one mile and you think you're at the other end of the earth. But you're not afraid; you know that what's gonna save you is the fact you're so little and everything around you's gonna get lost in its own bigness. When you get older and grown up then it's not the same at all. You walk down the streets an' think you're taller than the houses an' think the cars are goin' between your legs and think with a flick of your prick you could knock down every single one of the Steinberg's, and think everybody else is a dwarf an' if you wanted to you could scoop 'em up by the handfuls. But you don't use your powers; you wait for your moment an' you're too dumb to realize it's come an' gone an' you're gettin' worn down an' becomin' as little as everybody else which means one fine mornin' you wake up and find your legs limp as dish rags an' the bones broken an' stickin' out everywhere. What're you gonna do then? You go from pillar to post, try like hell to make ends meet and don't, or start yellin' or laughin' till you're out of breath, or else you just sit back an' watch yourself sink under. Don't worry! You're gonna wind up with a little pinhead and tiny arms and no feet an' no body an' no heart especially. No heart; the heart's important. No heart, you got no diamond or club or spade either. You're nothin' but a fuckin' lump of ground beef with raggedy legs that don't run that fast any more.) He'd opened all the doors now. He saw the blind television set in the living room under the plastic palm tree, he saw the monkey hanging from a branch, he saw the hollow cocoanut shell, he saw the frayed burlap trunk. Jeanne D'Arc had to really be angry for him to buy her a gift like that! (At Dupuis'.) And him drunk. Jeanne D'Arc was going to leave him because of the poke in the eye he gave her, because of the insults, because of the drinking, and him, he'd gone to Dupuis'. The taxi and the tree cost him his whole pay cheque, he must have explained all that to the salesman, who pretended not to hear, turning a deaf ear to those words oozing fear. Hey, listen you, you loaded or what? You don't understand nothin', eh? Then what you doin' here? He was acting that way out of impatience and out of brutal desire for Jeanne D'Arc lying on the sofa with a tiny bag of ice on her eye. Whew! It was a hard job gettin' all that

18

into the trunk of the car, alright. The memory made him terribly happy. He thought of the old taxi, the harsh lights, the screeching of the tires, the swarm of colors, buildings falling away behind the cars, the people, the nice-looking people walking up and down the streets, while the Pontiac was a half-tame animal let loose on Jeanne D'Arc's trail. (Ah, damn, damn!) And now there were just rooms which were too bare because Jeanne D'Arc wasn't in them. The dirt, the smell of burnt potatoes in the kitchen, of milk curdled in the container. And the living room. Jeanne D'Arc must have always watched television in the same spot, snuggled in a blanket in the rocking chair. The chair's rockers had left too many marks on the rug. And the potato chip crumbs, wasn't that proof enough? And the four coke bottles with the lipstick-stained straws. And the cigarette butts drowned in the bottles. Barthélémy remained perfectly still in the doorway. (Like on TV when they freeze the picture.) He felt nothing. His eyes were fixed in a stare and were filling up with water. A cordon of cops made an impenetrable curtain between him and the rest of the world. He was threatened and safe at the same time. If I was two people there'd be no problem. Each of us would have his place. Me, I could be mean an' him good. His ears tingled. The house was filling up with sounds, defending itself after its fashion against his intrusion; it was like a womb about to deliver, gas was escaping from it and it gave off cracking noises. How could Barthelémy not believe that he was once again a prisoner inside the white hospital where the only sounds were of needles piercing skin. He tried to move out of the doorway. Then suddenly everything went black. His knees buckled, his forehead struck the door frame, he fell on his leg (the dressing grew large and heavy with blood and pus and pain). He dragged himself down the hallway, grabbing at furniture. But running away was pointless because the guards were already at the door, the white guards were already blocking the windows — QUEBEC OCCUPIED. It was written in huge letters across the front page of the newspaper the guards brought him following his afternoon nap. (Why?) The nurses wore masks, they were naked but their faces were hidden behind squares of white gauze. The red rubber gloves. The frizzy, black hair below the belly. If it'd been any longer they'd have had real corkscrew curls. That's what he was thinking as the four nurses came towards him, he with a hard-on under the covers. They had tied him down to the bed, straps around his shoulders and knees; the nurses were really kangaroos or bloodsucking vampires. (Nothing escaped from that silent mouth.) Inside he was screaming and sirens were sounding. They took the sheet off the bed and tossed it aside, and the only vertical thing in that horizontal hospital world was his prick. The vampires were definitely going to grab him and plant passionate kisses all over him. Those teeth going into the skin. Those long draughts of blood, that prolonged sucking. Barthélémy doubled his efforts to move his trapped muscles. Warmth, and a heart bursting with love in his breast, and red tatoos on those impotent arms. Satiated, the vampires were perched on the big heating pipes which ran the length of the room. Other metamorphoses were going to take place, the vampires-kangaroos-nurses and the hypodermic needles would penetrate the flesh once again. Once again there would be inaudible cries and intense heat beneath the skin. During all this time Jeanne D'Arc's image pressing upon his eye, so small, so lovely, so pure. (Object of troubled affection rooted in the iris; a spear gouging the socket; blurred, failing sight.) Sphincters relaxing with rotten noises. Shitting and pissing. The white whale had strong breath. All around it a sheet of white, foul water in which the whaling ship was going to sink. The gold piece on the mainmast blinded Barthélémy. Unable to scream, he was crying. So, you like that book? Whales scare me. And cannibals more. The nurse was seated close by on the white chair taking his pulse. Those fingers with their long nails, and those protruding veins at his wrist, reassured him. I'm finished, eh? Why'd you have to kill me? The odor of excrement underneath him and this delicious feeling of buttocks wet with hot piss. He spit out the thermometer. You're acting like a child, monsieur Dupuis. Help us make you well. He kept his teeth clenched. His breath taken away because of the strap, his head like thunder ready to blow up the world. He would have liked to put his hand between the nurse's legs, violate her intimacy, get revenge for the indignities he was suffering. But she wasn't paying any attention to him now; the vampires had come back. They turned him over on his stomach and were holding his legs wide apart. His sex hurt him, his too-stiff prick was pure pain beneath him. Could the hippopotamus have put on the rubber glove the better to get inside him and brutally explore his anus? Don't you know it was time? You'd think there was cement in there. Oh, die of shame hearing the dry turds land in the bed pan. (Let go of me! Fuck, let go of me!) A car's headlights flashed yellow into the shadows, suddenly lighting up the long hallway. Barthélémy rubbed his eyes. He was covered with sweat, his leg was bloody and his heart beat rapidly in his chest. What the hell's happenin' to me? Heyheyhey! He lifted himself up and crawled on his knees to the door and collapsed on the porch beside his overnight bag. He was gasping for breath, tongue hanging out of his mouth, face on fire, blind and deaf and wild with excitement. Everything was turning, he couldn't tell where he was, there was too much wind and the flames were shooting out all around him now. He put his hand over his heart. Stop it, for God's sake! Stop it! He needed all his energy, something really serious must have happened while he was gone and if he didn't grab hold of himself he would be broken and destroyed before knowing what was what. He took a package of Forest out of his pocket, licked a Vogue paper, and came up with a pinch of tobacco. He was shaking so hard he lost the tobacco. His lungs were stopped up; there was no more air in the house, everything was crisp and dry. He made a sudden, violent movement with his body to break the spell and fell down the steps. Crying out – Jeanne D'Arc! Where are you, my Jeanne? He tried to get up. The back of his head struck something and all Barthélémy's strength left him. Later, he would understand that his head was stuck between two steps, that the wild grass growing beneath the porch was tickling his chin, and that he needed to laugh – It would rise on its own from somewhere deep within him, or maybe from somewhere outside him, so tired did he feel. Then the machines mounted him, caterpillar tractors flattening his back, jackhammers drilling his head; and, filling half the yard, there sat the grotesque hippopotamus, all smiles, its green teeth bared. Barthélémy couldn't keep from laughing, it made a protective wall between him and the rest of the world. I'll finally go to sleep. He wasn't aware right away of the importance of what he had just thought. He must have vomited before and wiped his lips on his shirtsleeve. Then he understood – that was the important word: sleep. He laid his head on the step and yawned. (Old lion lost in the jungle, mortally wounded, no Tarzan to bring him hunks of beef. Old fat-gut, toothless lion who's lost his roar. Go to sleep, damn it. Go to sleep. He knew Jeanne D'Arc would come back at the right moment, that first he had to wait for her deep in the heart of the night before he could take her in his arms. He let the tears flow down his cheeks and closed his eyes. He was floating down the Rivière des Prairies, gasping for breath, drowning in the blood running out of his leg) –))

CUT TWO

((And a long time after, when night was holding sway, blowing icy blasts of breath out over the world, Barthélémy slipped his hands down under his belt into his pants. Gotta keep warm. Can't afford to get cold. He was making his way through the snow, the toboggan cables cutting into his shoulders. Snot had frozen under his nose, while his hair, like all his bare head, was covered with ice. From time to time he stopped to catch his breath and would pull the toboggan to him. Stretched out under the blankets, Jeanne D'Arc was sound asleep. She's dead. Jeanne D'Arc's dead, can't you see? He would lift the blankets and look at the lifeless face, its eyes fixed in a stare and too wide open to see anything, then take off his mitten and put his hand on her cheek — the cold, all Morial Mort was frozen stiff beneath ice and wind. They were going to disappear under the snow, and the baby, stuck between Jeanne D'Arc's legs, would be a mongoloid, a water head whose birth would symbolize all that was hazardous, even impossible in the hoped-for survival of the world. Despite the shame, Barthélémy kept the cables on and continued to plow his way through the snow, driven forward by a will which wasn't really his: it was embedded in the very violence of the landscape. (You couldn't help but be tough when everything around you was.) Yet, he had few illusions: when the storm was over Jeanne D'Arc would be dead, the baby too, and he himself would be half-mad, a weathervane spinning before every kind of fear. I don't wanna stop, I wanna go on, I wanna go all the way to the end. The sled was sliding across the asphalt; the blades made sparks. Horrible

23

black birds were wheeling above the toboggan. The rotten flesh stank. What disgusted him most were the worms swarming over Jeanne D'Arc's face. Too much was being asked of him, they wanted to finish him off amid ugliness and horror. (Oh no, you sonsabitches, you ain't got my hide yet!) He opened his eyes. No, he couldn't sleep, too many thoughts were turning round in his head. He couldn't control them, make them go where he wanted them to go, make them submit, make them seem normal, which would have reassured him, quieted him down and left him in the old parents' big bed where, lying on his stomach in order not to see the demons in the window, he'd have gone to sleep with a finger in his mouth. Sleep, sleep, he repeated. He was trying to stay perfectly still there in front of the porch. Nothing, no doubt, but a shapeless body which had tumbled down the steps after tripping over the bag. Laughter was all that prevented him from being carried off in the downward swirl of the sinking whaler. Obviously that wasn't what he was thinking, his vision fell short of the Pequod, it didn't sail in his world, it was an unfortunate heel under which somebody standing over him would eventually crush him. Oh, he'd seen the film on television, alright, but he didn't remember the names; he'd been too busy naming what there was of Jeanne D'Arc once he'd undressed her. (Tits, bush, scum rag, ass, cunt, hole, cheese. Vocabulary to study closely. Words to get to know during the commercials, words to nose around in so memory might hold on to them and build him a past, that is, something solid he could pity the loss of once his Jeanne D'Arc had turned her back on him and left, because, she said, I'm gonna leave, you know I'm gonna leave one fine day. You damn fool, if you think I'm gonna spend my whole life with a boozer like you, well, you got your head up your ass an' I mean all the way up it. She said that time and time again. Sometimes adding: If I want to I can go out in that street an' say hi an' I'm off with the best lookin' pants in town, tailor made. You're nothin', Lémy. You've never had

24

me. Sometimes when you're on me I think of somebody else. An' course sometimes I can't think at all 'cause you get in my hair.) No doubt she was trying to be funny when she said that, and also, perhaps, she wanted to hurt him, and to make complicated things which didn't need to be. Laugh, mister, just go ahead and laugh. She would pretend she was watching television, her feet resting on the footstool, her face partially hidden behind her long, blond hair, her nails set wide apart on her thighs. But my Jeanne D'Arc, I love ya. I'm not such a bad guy after all, admit it. She wouldn't answer, her attention captured by the TV serial. Then she would assume a dangerous position (those legs spread terribly far apart to arouse him). She never wore underwear and there was too much life squirming in her crotch for Barthélémy not to be on fire. (Cut it out. Let me watch my program.) He wished she'd let him bother her, just some quiet pawing like putting a thumb a little way up her or some tit pinching with wet, shaky fingers, some tonguing in her ear or a few nibbles in that mass of bleached hair. Do you know what you want or not? 'Cause I'm not gonna be made a fool of like this all my life! Her indifference made him angry, he would walk back and forth in the kitchen opening one beer after another and talking to himself, sunk in drunkeness and sorrow. Pieces of sentences, unconnected words, confused noises coming into his mouth. The television stayed on till the wee hours of the morning, glittering greyly over the living room where Jeanne D'Arc would now be naked and cuddled up at the end of the sofa. All that time he was drinking and pacing the kitchen floor. He had an artificial leg made out of plastic and he had to keep his eyes on the holes the carpenter had drilled in the floor or he would topple over. He threw his cans and bottles in the back yard. Sometimes his aim was bad and he hit the pole they used as a banister for the back steps. The bottle would break and for a moment the noise drowned out the voices of the television actors. Then Jeanne D'Arc's shadow as she moved from the living room to the bedroom. (Come on, cute little Lémy. Come to mama. She's gonna give her Lémy some sweet milk.) He had to resist, he had to pay her back, push her down the stairs, slap her face, drive her stark raving mad, get rid of her forever. Weren't the cases of beer all empty now? One swallow left, two or three drops sent to reconnoitre down his gullet. After which he unfastened his suspenders, took off his pants and his old khaki shorts. No, I'm not goin', she can kiss my fuckin' ass, the crazy bitch! Tonight I'm stayin' in the kitchen. He sat down in the rocking chair with a hard-on a horse would have envied, his head full of filthy thoughts which made him ashamed. He crossed his legs to hide his prick. It was going to end badly, that was definite. (And Jeanne D'Arc's thighs opening and closing, wings of the fickle butterfly. Come on, old wolf-woof, come climb on your baby, come give her a hard dick. Gee, come on.) He was resisting; this wasn't the first time, he was used to spending his nights like this, wild-eyed and drunk and too alone to avoid the trap of obsession. But in all the time since he'd stopped sleeping nights he'd forgotten something. What was it? A gun, no doubt. He'd have cocked the rifle and stared down the liberating barrel all night. The hole the bullet would make between the eyes. (Come on, Lémy. I'm no tiger. You're a lot bigger than me.) She was soft now that the house was dark. But her voice was full of hatred. She's tryin' to make a fool outta me. An' she thinks she will. But she damn well won't! He'd never do a thing for her again. I've had just about enough of you, got that? He wasn't going to think of anybody but himself, of his stomach, his bad leg, of all he was going to drink and the jokes he'd tell to his old buddies, meaning Fred, Phil and Baptiste. His head hurt now that he was sobering up a little. He lit his flashlight. Nothin' but coke left. Lucky there's even that. He lifted off the cap, took a swallow and belched, feeling pleased with himself. He still told himself every now and then that he was somebody and that if his life was so full of ups and downs there must have been a reason for it, it wasn't his fault. I'll show'em what

I can do. At that same moment he thought of the bottle of aspirin in the medicine cabinet. (I'm goin' to sleep, Lémy. You're gonna come an' it'll be too late.) He swallowed the aspirin and drank the rest of the coke. He felt better right away and went back to the kitchen where, in the large, red chair he had made with his own hands, he began to rock rapidly and sing at the top of his lungs. If you don't pipe down I'm callin' the cops. (Kiss my ass, bitch!) They were no match for him, for his indignation and scorn. They were no match for his beauty and his strength. Come in here an' I'll punch you in the nose. He sat looking at his prick. (How many times had he let it ramble between Jeanne D'Arc's legs?) He was rocking too hard: the chair's rockers broke and he fell over backwards. A hard blow on the head, red stars, garbled sounds in his ears. He tried to get back to a kneeling position but saw he couldn't and stayed on all fours. There was something obscene in him, and great violence too. He arched his back like an animal against the table's chrome legs and out of his mouth came yelps or croaks (how to tell?). He'd gone to the shed and opened the can of tar and smeared it on generously. He was on fire. (Prick's hot as a damn clove.) He was moving on his hands and knees towards the bedroom where Jeanne D'Arc still lay pleading. (I'm gonna have to do it myself if you don't come give it to me, wolf-woof.) The closer he got to her the firmer he became in his deaf anger. She's gonna have a taste of it. He shot off a first time in the doorway, a powerful spray sending millions of mongoloids to their deaths. He placed a hand on the end of his prick; he felt intolerable joy and pain when his fingers landed. He still had a hard-on. He was a prick that had been hard too long. It was going to shoot out of every pore and flood Jeanne D'Arc like a prairie river in springtime. When I think it's been three months since I stuck it to you. You must be one hungry bitch! He was coming closer, nostrils flaring, sniffing. (The odor, the large, naked body on its back, the bouquet of black flowers between its legs. OK, Jeanne D'Arc, you win, I'm climbin' on.) He jumped into bed and threw Jeanne D'Arc's slippers on the floor. Then he started feeling her, his hands opening and closing like pliers on tits that refused to be caressed. If you're playin' a game, my Jeanne, why don't you tell me now. He was suffering, and furious about what he was being forced to do. He was being eaten alive with rage; he wept and screamed and threw punches wildly in the air. This was going to last a long time. Before it was over there'd be nothing left of his hands. And in fact when they were just bloody stumps he hid them under his body. Then he put his head between the two pillows and tried to sleep. He felt too heavy, he was overwrought, crazy. He was suffocating. His face was puffy and red. He needed to pee. (Hey, Jeanne, I'm back! Show a little interest, at least!) But there came no reply. Jumping up and down in the bed he felt like a kangaroo with boxing gloves on. He was sparring, making up left and right combinations as untold numbers of spectators throughout the arena applauded the punches landing with such accuracy on Jeanne D'Arc's face and neck and chest and lower abdomen. He had beaten her black and blue; swelling all over, she groaned as she asked forgiveness for her sins. Then a police car came slowly down the street. When Barthélémy saw it he took off his gloves and picked up Jeanne D'Arc's body and dumped it in the clothes closet. The cop car's red bubblegum machine was somehow still before his eyes. So he put on his pants hurriedly and lifted a corner of the curtain. The cops were parked across the street. Huge moths and other insects were swirling in the headlights' beam. (Are the fuckers gonna stay there all night???) Jeanne D'Arc was sobbing loudly in the closet and he was afraid the cops would come investigate, their night sticks drawn. They'd definitely let him have it with their sticks, even walk on him to cave in his ribs. He was trembling and couldn't take his eyes off the car. One of the cops had opened the door and put his leg out. Barthélémy released the curtain. (Seeing now only through the opening he made at the bottom of the

28

blind.) His teeth were chattering and his hands tugged violently at the curtain. The rod cracked then snapped in two. Barthélémy was caught in the wad of material that had fallen on his head. And that hand resting on his shoulder – or some monstrous paw that had caught him. So, to break the spell he threw himself against the window. The crash of glass, the cuts on his wrists, the thick blood covering his hands. He put his mouth over one of the wounds, and sucked. The ground was warm, and Jeanne D'Arc must have been dead now in the clothes closet. He didn't see the two cops cross the street and open the gate. He was thinking only of what it would be like when he ran out of blood. (What's goin' on here?) The cop struck him with his long stick between the shoulder blades. Barthélémy shook violently, all his muscles stiffening instinctively against the blows that were about to fall. (What the hell's the matter with you, fella?) The flashlight hurt his eyes. His mouth was full of blood and dirt, he couldn't talk. The cops made him get up and then sat him down on the bottom step. Now this interrogation again, this series of interchangeable questions. The cops had the same voice, nice and raucous. If you listened closely you could hear what was being said on the cop radio over the other sounds of the night. Barthélémy had to tell at length how he was coming back to the house after a long absence (unexplained) and how he was worried about Jeanne D'Arc. That's the little woman, understand. And that because he was in a hurry he had missed a step and fell. That was why he had yelled. The cops were looking at nothing in particular; maybe they had no eyes, just that tired, monotone voice. Yeah, well, you gonna have to keep it quiet, see? Barthélémy nodded energetically and stood up. The cops were already far away, the big automobile's motor made a lot of noise and the tires screamed a long time on the asphalt. With one swoosh the wind bent the trees at the end of the yard almost to the ground. God almighty, it's cold. Once inside the house Barthélémy turned off the television and the radio, then the lights, and, naked, got under the covers in the old parents' big bed. That's your wedding present, children. And where're you two gonna sleep then? Oh, no problem there. We'll spread some newspapers on the floor, they'll make a heck of a fine mattress. The old parents laughed, and he loved them for all the foolishness they made possible. (You know the one about the beggar who comes to the farmer's house late one night and asks them to put him up? Well, they didn't have a spare bed so they spread newspapers on the floor. The beggar didn't say anything: he undressed and wrapped himself in the pages of newspaper. During the night they heard a loud, strange noise but they were all afraid to get up and go see what it was. Morning came and everybody was sitting down at the big table for breakfast; they asked the beggar if he'd heard anything the night before. Well, the old boy said, yeah, I know I made noise, and I'm sorry; I fell out of bed!) Hee-hee-hee-hee went Barthélémy. Hands behind his head, his eyes open wide, he had told that story to himself often. (I was a little tiny thing but I was nobody's fool.) He stretched his legs and pushed his toes between the bars of the bedstead. The pulsing blood at his temples would eventually put him to sleep. But to sing a lullaby was quicker. His disturbing voice sent the shadows scurrying back against the walls. Barthélémy rolled over on his stomach and stuck a finger in his mouth. He didn't know why he'd broken into the house and why he'd tied up the beautiful Jeanne D'Arc and put her in the clothes closet. He especially wondered why he had undressed and come to bed. He turned these questions over in his mind several times but found no answers to them. Something wasn't right but he couldn't tell what it was. The world lay beyond his reach, he was cut off from it. He was the old carcass of some wild beast they'd taken axes to. He growled. He wasn't going to be beaten so easily. I'll show Jeanne D'Arc I'm no crazy sick man you can put away! He threw the covers to the foot of the bed. I can't sleep these days. What's a man gotta do, goddamn it! At the start of his illness, when

Jeanne D'Arc wasn't by his side he got to sleep by softly patting his hands together. But now nothing coming from him brought any reassurance at all. I'm just out of it. Sobs in the clothes closet. Barthélémy listened carefully. Was the demon still there, to obsess him till his dying day? He sat up in bed chewing his thumbs. He knew he couldn't resist the temptation: soon he would leap out of bed in a rage and go open the closet door and find Jeanne D'Arc soaked in blood. I'm gonna rip your guts out if you don't stop whining! He did nothing to stop the anger rising in him because to act he needed to feel its terrible compulsion. What he was going to do was odious and asked for a lot of courage. How quiet everything was! And how peacefully everything was dying! He reached for the bottle of coke on the dressing table and yanked open the drawer. The bottle of aspirin emptied in the mouth – and washing them down with a few good swallows of carbonated water. Tears came to his eyes, an intolerable pain bore into his head. Then he went into a trance and slid off the old parents' big bed onto the floor. He moved on all fours across the rug and sniffed the slippers that Jeanne D'Arc must have forgotten in her hurry to leave. The slippers stank of beer or vomit. He had to stop himself from throwing up. Then he farted noisily. It only excited him more. He was a bulldozer rumbling through the bedroom. Then he stuck his behind against the chest of drawers and pushed as hard as he could. Its legs scratched the floor. Now able to move between the wall and chest of drawers, Barthélémy opened hs mouth and the terrifying roars blew out the window panes. The game was no longer being played according to the rules, even though the stage was set and the bit players, as one body, were taking the places assigned to them by what Barthélémy in his dream called, since he couldn't come up with anything better, The Mouth. All you had to do was look at the tablet hanging on the bedroom door: one chalk mark meant a table, two a chest of drawers, three the life-sized, inflatable doll symbolizing impure Jeanne D'Arc, four marks

31

the invisible, all mighty demons whose job it was to watch what would happen before brutally intervening. Barthélémy was still crawling. He wasn't thinking of what he was going to do: his brain was absolutely dead and cold. There was only a thin stream of memory flowing from his eyes now, reminding him of the numerous rehearsals for the show he would soon put on. But at Dorémi the hall was larger and the lighting better. Here Barthélémy had the feeling he was playing in the sticks before country bumpkins who, when the show got violent, would rise to a man and protest. (And how was he going to be able to duck the rotten tomatoes and stumps of cabbage?) For a moment he remained still, one leg hiked up, his long, soft prick lost in pubic hair. His body broke out in a sweat, he had to close his eyes; the spotlights blinking on and off so fast panicked him. I won't be able to. I'm too sick. The weight of his body rested on one leg. The leg began to tremble and Barthélémy fell. The noise his bones made crashing against the open dresser drawer made him think he had just been knocked on the head. Had they just mutilated him horribly and were they now going to force him to crawl through the sawdust to render him ridiculous? He managed to reach Jeanne D'Arc's dead body hanging at the back of the freezer. He was crying, sobs stuck in his throat and nothing frightened him more than to see, in the ripped-open body, the four empty beer bottles somebody had put there. He rolled around in the garbage. In spite of the cold her body was rotting. Her cheeks were already missing, and hadn't The Mouth just taken off a chunk of the hind quarter for a customer? (The freezer was pitching, it was that old boat in the book sinking in the ocean miles from the white whale. And they were chopping him up in little pieces − Oh, The Mouth's big moustache. The Mouth's veined skin. The Mouth's warts. Why did they want to terrify him by chopping him up in the meat grinder?) (And how could he have kept from screaming?) The palms of his hands were burning, there was only fire, just a trail of flames writhing in the sawdust. The show. I've gotta think about the show and nothin' else. (Improvise! screamed a voice in his ear.) He didn't know why all the patients at Dorémi had put on white robes and were carrying tall, lighted candles: they were coming towards him chanting, their eyes half-closed, possessed by an alien force. He was surrounded, the candle flames were almost touching him, blisters rose on his skin, they wanted to kill him, he couldn't stay there impassive, clenching his fists wasn't enough. He began to kick. The Mouth exploded like thunder in his head: I told you to be faithful to the story. A good actor's somebody who can do things he couldn't do in real life. OK, Boss. He fell flat on his face after being kneed in the kidneys. They were going to walk on him, crush his hands, set his hair on fire. I won't be able to stand that. I'll explode first. He closed his eyes and let the patients strike him. He was covering his head with his large hands and screaming desperately. His cries didn't carry very far, didn't break through the circle the other patients made around him. His body was oozing pain from every pore. (Writhe, collapse, break, lie contorted, bleed, no complaints, believe stubbornly in what was becoming just so much liquid flowing down under the floor boards.) Just a second. He thought of the chain around his neck. He didn't understand why he hadn't taken it off before the show started. He should have known that tempers would get hot, that the patients would lose control as they brusquely demanded roles worthy of them. To kill, yes, that was what they wanted: to kill him, kill him traitorously, to put him to death so that justice should be sanctified and tolerable. He began to squeal like a pig, anguished cries which should have convinced the patients that they had the wrong man and that he couldn't possibly be the one they were looking for. (I'm not the one that fucked everything. Not me! I'm with you, we're buddies, right Phil? Right, Fred? Right, Baptiste? Right, Thérèse? An' I ain't said nothing to the guards. My whole life I've kept my mouth shut, I don't see why I'd open it now that I'm in prison. I hate 'em as much as you. They could stick me all they wanted, I kept my mouth closed tight an' nothin' got out.) He knew there was no use his trying, nobody wanted to listen. But perhaps he was doing it precisely because it was impossible, and more than impossible, because in so doing he was signing his death warrant. He hardly moved when the patients took hold of his legs and dragged him into another room, one a lot smaller than the first. They laid him on a kind of altar. He saw right away what they were up to: there was a trap door which they could open any time they wanted with a hidden lever. After they'd finished choking him with the chain. And weren't the patients going to take out a small package of Gilette blades and ferociously attack his leg? There was also the fact that the patrol car was once again in front of the house, and had been for a while. Barthélémy hid his head in his hands. What he'd seen had disgusted him. The bedroom was turned upside down now. He'd turned over all the furniture, emptied all the drawers, ripped up Jeanne D'Arc's clothes with his teeth, broken the lamps, gutted the mattress. (Now the red flashes of the cop car's blinking bubblegum machine.) His nerves were on edge and an atrocious fear had taken hold of him. The big dog was there, his yellow paws on his shoulders. Fetid breath, a rough tongue licking his unshaven cheek, malicious eyes. (How could you free yourself from all that when the night was proceeding with such anarchy.) The cops must have been knocking at the door. Hearing the noise, the big dog let his paws fall to the floor. His ears pricked up. The dog barked loudly before disappearing into the hall. He would get out of the house by the open window at the back of the kitchen and hide behind the pumpkins. Barthélémy heard the two men's voices and the porch creaking beneath their feet. The door wouldn't hold for long. He dived under the bed, striking his head against the iron bedstead. Nothing had ever scared him as much as what he thought he saw coming. Weren't the cops going to come in the house? Weren't the cops going to snoop around and look under this bed where he was hiding, his teeth chattering? In those knuckles rapping against the glass there was violence which bode ill. He'd have had to flee right away, do like the big yellow dog and run away into the night. The noise the door panes made, a quick series of ultimatums which he could only answer by silence and his will to stand fast. With the help of a key he'd taken out of his pocket he began to lift off the layers of brass which had been laid (oh, how many years ago now?) on the legs of the old parents' big bed. His fear had given him the hiccups. Acting like this, that was how he'd finally forget the policemen and maybe even really start to wait for his Jeanne D'Arc. (But why the hell did he have to wait so long?) —))

CUT THREE

((And he wept, overwhelmed by the beauty of the scene. She was walking so daintily on her tiptoes, swinging that large ass so gracefully. When she let herself go how affectionate she was, how closely she resembled him. So they made the game more complicated, switching roles, she putting on his pants and he her flowery dress. But tits, I don't have any tits, Lémy. Her ass was wondrous to behold, a sheer delight which sent him reeling with happiness. Saying, My tits Lémy, I've gotta have tits if I'm gonna be you. She was circling him slowly in her male disguise. The padded bra dangling from her fingertips looked like two enormous red eyes – they had just ripped them out of the monster's head in the basement. Then she helped him into the halter. You're a real women now except for the bushy hair under your arms. A woman shaves. We're gonna have to take it off, eh? She nodded: Yeah, you're right, mister. I ain't Jeanne D'Arc yet. She let him run to the bathroom and he came back with a razor, shaving cream and lotion. I think if I was to lie down and put my arms behind my head it'd be a hell of a lot better. She trusted every word he said. Shaking the can of shaving cream and pressing the button, she thought of cops arriving unexpectedly, but wasn't really worried. The white foam was cold in his armpits. I should've cut the thick parts with the scissors first. With the razor I'm gonna scrape your under-arms. She went back to the bathroom. The tap made noise, all the pipes in the house shook because of the heavy gases. The damn things're about rusted away. She came right back. The wet washcloth flattened the hair down into the folds of the skin. Above Jeanne D'Arc's head the scissors shone brightly. Why this need to make the pleasure last by clicking the scissors in thin air? Hey look, a little bird, a kingfisher, divin' into the Rivière des Prairies an' comin' up with a big fish all covered with shit. Then she moved her arm quickly and the scissors became a bolt of lightning striking the floor. Do it quick, kid, my arms're gettin' tired. I'm gonna have one hell of a cramp if you don't hurry up. So she pulled the scissors loose and leaned over what in a moment would metamorphose into Jeanne D'Arc. Too bad you don't have a moustache, I'd throw a scissors hold on it before you knew it. Now, there was a question of Barthélémy's voice. It wasn't Barthélémy's voice. It was higher, weaker, it hurt your ears. But she didn't let that bother her. As far as she was concerned everything was fine, the identification couldn't be more complete; her mouth wasn't failing her in what it actually said – even Barthélémy might have been fooled. Now she'd cut all there was to cut with the scissors. She straightened up, gripping a handful of rust-colored hair. She went and put it in the ashtray, and, holding up her pants, came back to the new Jeanne D'Arc. She kissed Jeanne D'Arc's armpits because she was satisfied with him and wanted her to know it. She answered these caresses with whimpers and began to finger the other's zipper; five pricks felt around in dark fleece. As she raised her head and looked between her legs, she thought, I'm a woman but do I ever have a hard on! Her tits hurt. My tits always hurt real bad when I'm about to have my period. And this pain in the ovaries (was that what it was?). Christ! Christ! Ream me, she said to the new Jeanne D'Arc who was letting herself be carressed on the mons veneris. (Oh, how good it was to be a woman so the five pricks of the fake Barthélémy's left hand could commit their indiscretions in the majestic crack!) Then saying, Take me in your arms and carry me around your house, the big world of your house. But you're too heavy, honey. She wanted him to try nonetheless. What you gotta do is hold me tight so I can feel your fingers in my flesh. We're gonna die, my Lémy. Hey, do you always think about things like that? But that's what I feel. I feel like we're just about finished. That it won't be long now. So you want me to kill myself for my Jeanne D'Arc??? She touched his stomach, saying, Kill me first, kitten. I've gotta feel you way up inside me. That's why we had to switch places. But now I don't wanna play any more. I don't like it. An' I'm really worn out. The new Jeanne D'Arc was ill at ease. She wasn't used to wearing a cumbersome brassière, the heavy padding hurt her chest. If you don't carry me around the house, I'm just gonna leave you to yourself. In Barthélémy's voice, she said, OK Jeanne D'Arc, my love. I'll carry you around the house. But give me time to catch my breath. And she said also, Your hand won't keep still and it's too deep in my pants. She'd have liked to add: Will it be in your skin that I'll find true pleasure for the first time? But she didn't know such words. There was only the confused desire to say them, which welled up in her as tears came to her eyes. Now don't start cryin'. Come on. You wanna ruin the play? She (or he since it was really dark now, so dark in fact that all they could see in each other's faces was a little of the white of their eyes; it was becoming difficult to take one for the other and the maliciously changed voices made it all the harder — she, then, stood still by the bed, giving herself up to her pleasure as she made a first move: she leaned over the other suffering in the brassière and violently jerked his dress up over his head. Then she began to take the throbbing prick's pulse. I don't want you to beat me off, I want you to carry me in your arms around the house. No surprise. You never let me do that to you. She didn't finish this impossible sentence; she didn't even have time to formulate it because her sex was being tickled too hard by the five pricks, lapping like tongues, of the left hand of what looked too much like Barthélémy to be true. She had to squirm and writhe standing in place and remember throughout her orgasm to hold her pants up with one hand. Because if she let herself get carried away and

39

forgot that detail it would cost her dearly, this new Jeanne
D'Arc. She was all too familiar with the impromptu rages. She
couldn't be getting herself punched in the nose everyday. (It
was a sacrilege to watch television through only one eye.) So
she cut short the sacred contractions and moved away from
the new Jeanne D'Arc's wet hand. Here I come, ready or not.
She made clucking noises and them imitated the sound of the
Boeings' eight big motors over Morial Mort when they're
getting ready to become large birds of ill omen. And, in fact,
at about the same moment two turbo jets landed right under
her body, which she'd taken care to lift so their noses
wouldn't break her ribs. She was lying stretched out and
relaxed in the old parents' big bed while the spitting image of
Barthélémy moved into position. She was breathing hard,
her buttocks were trembling, and she didn't know how she'd
managed to lift the motionless mass by the name of the new
Jeanne D'Arc and not let the pants fall. Maybe it ain't important. Because of what's involved maybe she won't notice. But
unfortunately she couldn't be certain. (And the huge fist and
the Death's Head ring were already looming into her dream,
or her memory, she wasn't sure which.) And that murderous
presence which was going to come, or which had already
come, so terrified her that she didn't notice that Barthélémy
was growing impatient and pulling her hair. Her hands came
alive again only when she heard, Listen, you waitin' for the
fuckin' messiah? She went into action, putting off till later
trying to have answers to her questions, letting the darkness
seize her. She was afraid Barthélémy was no longer Barthélémy all of a sudden nor the version of herself he had been.
In such darkness anything could happen. At least when I'm
alone I leave the night light on. She tensed her muscles so
she'd be able to lift the man-serpent out of bed. Hold yourself stiff, Lémy. She panted while he cursed. You ain't worth a
damn as an actress! Understand once an' for all that you're
Barthélémy and I'm Jeanne D'Arc. Look at me, I got the
brassière an' the falsies an' the dress. What more do you

want? An' you, you got the pants. She was dying of shame. She wasn't able to do what he asked. She wondered sillily why everything wasn't simple between them; and she reflected that she'd be happy just to spread her legs and get it the usual way. He's gettin' a little too weird for me. An' I'm just about to tell'im so. They closed their eyes in order not to see the patrol car which sped past the house. It wasn't going to stop this time. They both listened to the siren's shrill scream as it sounded over their heads to oppress them. Thinking of Jeanne D'Arc, Barthélémy's hands became fists; soon, wasn't she going to call the cops to get shut of him? Yeah, we're gonna take a little break and then pick up where we left off. OK? Still out of breath, she didn't answer. Her two hands were inside her pants. She wondered how it was she had five pricks on each hand and none between her legs. As for Barthélémy, he was suffering because of his bad leg and the false tits which, high on his chest, felt like two heavy, brass balls. His lungs were burning and he coughed flames a long time trying to clear them. −))

CUT FOUR

((After that, he crouched down, breathing hard, rage coming back. He narrowed his eyes to better observe the contemptible, inert form next to him. Tell me about Fred. Lémy, no, not that; not that, no. I wanna know everything, OK? I wanna know what you were doin' with Fred while I was locked up in Dorémi. Out with it, damn it. Out with it! I ain't been waitin' for you all night for nothin'. He slapped her. Jeanne D'Arc opened her mouth. I can't tell you all that; you'll kill me. He slapped her again. Why was he so keen on her going over it yet another time? He knew just what had happened. First, the big car had come flying down des Récollets Street; then screeched to a halt; then Fred had reached over and grabbed her and pulled her to him and kissed her on the mouth. Had done more than that, in fact. The man had boldly hiked Jeanne D'Arc's dress up to her waist (earlier, during the night, when the car was traveling down narrow, deserted roads, he'd told her to take off her panties, roll her dress up to her stomach and spread her legs wide so the wind blowing through the convertible would caress her fluff, so as he drove he could take it all in for the first time) — but now they were back, the odyssey was ending in front of the old parents' big house. And Jeanne D'Arc's buttocks, fat, beautiful buttocks, had sweated a lot; the flesh stuck to the leatherette, separating from it noisily. Just as the leatherette squeaked when Jeanne D'Arc, tickled by the man's finger, moved her legs, spreading them even wider to get as much pleasure as possible, so that the sight of that ready and willing cunt would make the man go wild and not know any longer what he was doing, stepping down hard on the accelerator, one hand holding the steering wheel while the other opened his fly, pulled down his underwear and lifted out of that ridiculous, tweedy clump his juicy, sticky, swollen, enormous prick. He had definitely stopped the big car on the side of some dark road, cutting the motor and then, right after, the lights. Maybe they'd even rolled up the windows because of the mosquitoes, ignoring the fact that it was hot on the lowered leatherette seat. It made a soft bed, and Jeanne D'Arc was thinking as the man undressed her, nibbling her tits and, moments later, the tiny rolls of flesh at her waist, and the mons veneris certainly, sucking the pubic hair, the searching tongue like a tender prick: and the man's hollow words (I'll love you forever, my Jeanne, my love): and the waves, so many waves in which to be caught up and sent tumbling head over heels: crying out and grabbing those balls, huge nuts, painful and full of blood – during all of it Jeanne D'Arc had thought how good it would be if she could feel the man moving up and down on her forever, if love's pump never stopped; and how of the fingers stuck far up her ass, the hand lifting her buttocks, the soft music on the radio; how of everything on her and above her, those feet propped against the back seat, the heavy, rhythmical breathing, the salty sweat, and that prick inside her moving faster and faster, hurting her more and more as it went deeper and deeper, the intensified pleasure (she was a rubber sling and the man's prick a large stone stretching her and twisting her out of shape, sending tremors through her); how soon of all of that there'd be nothing left but this large mouth open wide just above her face, this yellow mouth that was going to devour her. Oh oh oh oh oh! howled Jeanne D'Arc. Make it last forever, let the car drive itself and let everybody in our provinces and territories, and in the United States, let the French and the Savages and the British and the Métis see us naked and right in the middle of fornicating, sweaty, out of our minds with pleasure, let it serve as an example and once that's

44

done nothing'll be impossible. (Her pleasure was a masked devil with a buffalo's horns, a buck's eyes, a pig's snout and thick, nigger lips, wearing skins and sporting long necklaces made of real boors' teeth. Her pleasure was a wild deer-devil, his belling rang in her ears, causing her to fling herself into hell. Her pleasure was turning her into an accordion, her body beneath the man's now stretching, now folding. Barthélémy could drop dead!) And so what if you're in the window lookin' and waitin' for me like an asshole, your dick hangin' down between your legs. It's too late, Lémy! I'm never comin' back, you're just rottin' away. What d'you want me to do, I can't spend the rest of my life takin' care of you, I'm no nurse, for Christ sake. I've had it. The other day when you had your attack there I was all day long washin' your feet an' givin' you your shots and changin' your bandages an' undressin' an' cleanin' you — no, no, no! I can't do it any more, Lémy! Get that through your head! You're finished, an' me, I'm full of life. Go to sleep, Lémy, go to sleep. The car would never stop rolling through the night. They would get to the Pie ix bridge soon and perhaps the first workers would already be there strapped into their safety belts high up on the girders over the Rivière des Prairies, two hundred feet in the air, screwing in gigantic bolts. The man was driving with one hand. With the other he was caressing Jeanne D'Arc's tit. She was snuggled against him, half-naked and still warm with all the love his fast-moving prick had left in her. She was almost asleep, her tongue between her teeth. How could the man not find her beautiful there by his side? I'll pull up an' you get out; I'll pretend to leave but I'll stop just down the street an' wait. If Barthélémy gives you any trouble I'll come an' kick his ass. She'd opened her eyes; she was so tired she could hardly hear what he was saying. In any case, Barthélémy wasn't going to do anything; since his leg had begun to give out little by little, he didn't dare hit her. I'm stronger than he is now. I can set him on his behind with the back of my hand. Forget it, Fred.

Besides, when you let me off at home, I'm home. The man growled. I don't like it. I don't like you stayin' with a guy like that. You never know. She shrugged her shoulders and bent down and picked up the red panties she had slipped off earlier. She saw the heavy, dull brown stain. The man let go of her tit, reached and took the panties. Jeanne D'Arc thought of the baby, that sticky thing, dead when it came out of the womb, and of the cord which had kept her tied for too long to death. (Baby cold in the snow, baby stiff between her legs. Where and when? On what white road?) Death had come from her loins as she lay screaming, death had come gushing out of her in shame and in fear. Destroy. Cast into the cold this death conceived as she lay crushed beneath Barthélémy's body, her head filling up with stars and fire. And cry because of the fruitless past and the armless, legless baby who made the future impossible. Once a boozer always a boozer, I may be cracked but I can hold it. Barthélémy saying such things, laughing and singing as he stowed the stolen quart jars of nails safely away behind the old skin cover. Barthélémy, the good old Barthélémy of the time before the cold baby, before the first kick in the gut — *that* Barthélémy was always singing. You don't know how much I wish he'd died before he got sick, Fred. Nothin's left from before. Is it gonna last much longer, I wonder? Her head was resting on the man's shoulder; she wanted to cry, it was as though her head were suddenly full of water. But the tears didn't come. Too much pleasure had been had that night. She was caressing the man's thigh softly. And he was still holding the panties. He sniffed them, looked at the stain and the black hairs, then breathed in deeply to force as many odors as possible down into his lungs. He'd done the same thing with all the women he'd seduced. (That was the most important part of the first night: taking possession of the odors.) (Smelling a lot created the essential tie.) She watched him doing it, her hands between his legs, two fingers placed in the open zipper. A little while before she wouldn't have let the man bury his nose in her panties. But now she allowed it as a way of forgetting Barth-élémy and of coming back to what was being lived in the car. Perhaps the panties were a form of revenge against Barth-élémy. Put them on, said the man. I've gotten all the smells there are to get. There was the bridge and dawn come too early. He handed her the panties. When his hand was free he placed it on Jeanne D'Arc's, which she had left between his legs, her fingers holding his stiff, moist, twitching prick. The bridge, he said. He removed her hand and put his prick back in his pants and zipped them up. He wiped away the white stain on his pants with his handkerchief. Jeanne D'Arc had stepped into the panties as the man drove on, watching her. The panties stopped at the thighs and Jeanne D'Arc supported herself with her feet and the small of her back as she raised her buttocks and pulled the panties over the small scar on her belly. Afterwards, the man kept his eyes on the road; the closer they came to the bridge the heavier the traffic. They had to slow down. Everyone had to consider the possibility of a bottleneck at the entrance to the bridge, and deal with the huge trucks parked alongside the road, and with the noisy cranes whose winches, loaded with steel beams, were swinging over their heads. (Could you roll up your window? I'm cold, Fred. Sure, sweetie. You shouldn't call me that, Fred. I always think you're laughin' at me when you call me that. No, no, no.) In spite of it all, she had smiled at him, happy to be at his side, next to that soft strength. She would have liked so much for the night not to end so she and Fred could keep going through the darkness. They'd have followed Pie ix Boulevard, running the red lights, and then taken the Metropolitan east to Lafontaine Tunnel where the radio wouldn't work any more, there'd be so much static they'd have to turn it off. Water would be seeping through the walls, running down into pools on the asphalt. The deafening noise of the pile drivers, the yellow bubblegum machines and blinkers of the roads department trucks parked on both sides of the highway. And high above them a long stretch of water with its fish, its flotsam and jetsam, the sunken boulders along its sides, the oil slicks and those large boats gliding calmly through the Saint Lawrence. (Do we keep goin' or d'you want me to take you back?) She had answered that she wanted to look some more, that Morial seen from the highway by the river didn't look at all like she'd imagined it would, it was nice, what with so many lights and colors, and here and there a pink or blue neon sign blinking like an eye. (Night swallowed by artifice, black, red, black, yellow, green, like the beating of a heart.) (Maybe the lighted signs were really metal sorcerers planted over the roofs to pacify the night's evil forces and prevent them from taking over the city.) What're you thinkin' about? asked Fred. I'm lookin', I think it's really nice. She leaned over and kissed him on the cheek several times. The man's hair was slicked down at his grey temples and smelled of brilliantine. The large hands on the steering wheel were comforting. The tiny blue eyes beneath those eyebrows made her warm all over, she was radiant with happiness. She had asked, Do you really love me, Freddy? Had he grimaced slightly? Hey, you know I do. He'd turned his head and kissed her quickly on the lips. Don't always think about what's gonna happen, think about what's happenin' now, at the present moment. He pressed down on the accelerator and the tires squealed. The Jacques Cartier bridge was just ahead, intimidating with its carcass of metal and light. Bedoom, bedoom, bedoom, said Jeanne D'Arc each time the tires went over a grating. It was false dawn now, the river was hidden beneath a thick layer of fog. I've gotta get back, said Jeanne D'Arc. We'll be there soon, little girl, he said. She didn't especially like the fact that he talked to her like a child, but she was already getting tired of saying so. Maybe she just had to get used to it. In speaking that way he must have been expressing desires he'd kept inside for too long. So be easy, she thought. So what if you're bein' taken for a ride. She laughed out loud. I'm bein' taken for a ride – in a Buick. She found her handkerchief and blew

48

her nose. You're in good spirits, my Jeanne, said the man. I'm happy, that's all. Me, too. She leaned her head back on the leatherette seat and closed her eyes so as not to see the day break. It was all happening so fast that she hadn't had time to really put her past behind her now that the night had brought her everything she wanted. (It was the rustling of the leaves, the night birds, the indiscernible movements in the dark, the wind, the bare foot planted in a soft cow turd, it was more that than the man's being on top of her, more that than his being anchored in that ocean between her legs. It was so good! she reflected.) The man had pushed the lighter button on the dashboard; she couldn't see him but she knew him well enough after only one night to tell what he looked like sitting there with his forearm held close to his face, nose itching because of the smoke. Why keep from crying now that Morial Mort was coming towards her, its claws out? Fred, honey, it's already autumn. Want a drag? he asked. She shook her head no, facing in the direction of the cold and of the snow that was going to fall in the dry, leafless world, in the icy, icy, icy world. She felt bad; she shivered. Cling, cling to the man, to his lie, hold off the first heavy snow. You asleep? asked the man. No, no, Freddy, I'm just tired. She would have liked to say, oh it's happy tiredness, but the idea just touched her lightly like the end of the man's cigarette when he put his hand on her neck. Let's stop, she had said when they had almost reached the end of Saint-Michel Boulevard. What for? No reason, Freddy, no reason. He put his foot on the brake and the tires scraped against the curb. He looked at her. There was that same softness in the man's eyes. Get out and walk, and run, even, before the Italians and the children in the school yard, and Morial Mort should come with the sun and the day's confusion, and Fred himself, who had accompanied her through the night, should be caught up in it. Can I talk to you about Lémy? She knew very well he didn't want her to, but because of what Barthélémy had done to her, had been doing to her for so many years, she

49

couldn't keep it inside her any longer either. She yawned and played with her wrist watch. She felt the tears come into her eyes. She pressed her body hard against the man's and began to sob. She wasn't saying the right things: the words gushing from her mouth were endangering her, chasing the man away, and failed to deliver her from the pain Barthélémy caused her. He caressed her hair in silence, counting simply on the strength of his gentleness to console her, to take her away from Barthélémy, to get her out from under his spell. It wasn't the first time he'd had to do something like this for her. Later he'd tell her that the scene had made his head spin. There was Barthélémy hidden behind the stretch of quart jars of nails; he'd just beaten Baptiste unconscious; and the woman was crying, Jeanne D'Arc was crying, blinded by the blood flowing from the wound Barthélémy had caused over her eye when he struck her with the wrench; and the man she called Fred had appeared in the doorway, then come down the basement steps, deafened by the screams and sobs. Fortunately he'd had the flashlight in his hand and so was able to follow its yellow light and, at the same time, let them see him, they who a few feet ahead were crawling in dirt and blood and urine. Police! Police! Police! he had cried, turning the flashlight's beam on the star on his chest. Then, with the two other cops pushing him from behind, he'd gone forward, knocking over the quart jars of nails, and grabbed Barthélémy's wrist. It all happened fast, surrounded by the smell of home brew which had been spilled in the dirt. Barthélémy was threatening him with the wrench but he'd had no trouble overpowering him. He had twisted his arm and held him fast before handing him over to another cop. (Let's go, motherfucker, come on, get up those steps! A few kicks in the leg maybe, and a few harder blows in the kidneys. Move, bastard, move!) He had gone to see about the woman lying among the broken bottles. The flashlight's beam came to rest on the bare, bloody ass, and why the hell did he let himself be taken in by those cunning curves, those cunt hairs peeping up from between the white buttocks? He'd wiped her face, saying banal things to calm her. Then he'd helped her to her feet and up the steps. (Remembering all of that and what had followed, that is, the conversation in the kitchen, the questions asked for the report.) When had he remembered the wounded eye and called for the first aid kit? When, since she was crying because the lights were harsh, did he have them turned off for her, all except the one in the kitchen? And when especially had she taken his hands and pressed them against her chest? Jeanne D'Arc's nipples, the fingers not moving at first but the temptation too strong, and before long the caresses, those white, swollen tits in his hands. The chair legs had squealed when the two of them stood up; he had taken her in his arms, she was sobbing and shaking violently as she leaned against him (and that eye now hidden behind a wad of cotton, the eyebrow hairs stuck under tape). He had wondered for a moment whether she was all there or not, maybe she was a crackpot; but the sight of those tits, the dress sliding down off her shoulders when he unhooked it, the night delivering her up to him like this, all this white flesh, it was too beautiful. They were standing in the kitchen, she was supporting herself against the table (what joke had he made about the large buttocks on the pink arborite?); his legs were spread wide apart, he was holding his breath, resisting the raw, brutal obscenity of what was rushing through his mind (why not grab an ass that grabs you?). She'd taken off his cap and put her hand on his prick which was stiff inside his pants. Kiss me, Fred, kiss me. Despite the dried blood under her nose he did as she asked. The tongue penetrating the soft mouth, finding pools of saliva, tickling the uvula. The hands spread wide, grabbing, grabbling, grappling with that ass. She had unzipped his pants, pulled down his shorts and taken his prick between her fingers. Then. A few more caresses on the head of his prick (why had she wet it with spit?). Give it to me, Freddy, give it to me. I need it bad. That was how it had all started, and now he was kissing her tearful eyes, his big car's motor running slowly. The traffic light: now green, now red, now yellow. She no longer counted the changes as she did when she was small and fascinated by the electric light hanging over the street. Why don't you leave Barthélémy? Fred asked. You know everything'd be alright at the house, I'd take good care of you. The loud kiss went crashing into the window. (To explain why wasn't easy. Fred would have had to live in the old parents' big house with Barthélémy and her from the beginning to understand. Basement. Nails. Harmonica. Old buddies. Baptiste. Pumpkins. Big yellow dog. Without these things how would life be possible, how could she keep a grip on it?) The car drove away amid Fred's silence. They turned, raising dust off the sidewalk. The car was a red arrow shot straight down the still streets. Soon both Jeanne D'Arc and Fred would drop from fatigue. She let him kiss her in front of the house even if she knew Barthélémy was looking out from behind the bedroom curtain, filing his nails. (Fuckin' bitch! Slut! Go ahead, keep talkin' or you'll get a fist in the mouth!) She had nothing to add. She couldn't tell Barthélémy that in that car-bed parked on the deserted road, Fred, naked, had stuck his prick in her mouth and that she'd done everything asked of her — the skin peeled back, the buttocks, and what had come, all his white softness spurting against her teeth as he held her against him, gripping her neck and forcing her head to remain against his thighs. And then he too, he'd spread her legs, and taken a trick rubber statue out of the glove compartment; seen from one side it was Saint Joseph, from the other a splendid prick; and Fred had put it between her legs and they'd played some strange games. (Tall beautiful bitch and a well-hung hunk.) Come on, tell me, Goddamn it! But I told you everything, Lémy. Forgive me. Never! I'm gonna lock you in the clothes closet! No, Lémy, not that. No, no, no! I'll do anything you want —))

CUT FIVE

((She took Barthélémy in her arms, breathed deeply, and, unsteady on her feet, began the long voyage around the house. Sing. It doesn't work, if you don't. She opened her mouth and murmured, Oh, oh, big baby blue, oh, oh, big baby blue. He let her do what she wanted because he'd been waiting days and days for this, for these signs of tenderness, this loving simplicity he'd missed so much at Dorémi in the white ward where he was held prisoner by the hippopotamus. (Was his Jeanne D'Arc aware of what soothing beauty they were capable, when he acted decisively and forced her to be herself?) Oh, oh, big baby blue in his mama's arms, oh, oh, big baby blue in his mama's arms, oh, oh. (These sung blues opening a tap of limitless mutual affection. These blues which were turning Jeanne D'Arc into Barthélémy.) Oh, oh, big baby blue, oh, oh, big baby blue. She was singing to be nice to him, and also, no doubt, to console him; he was so weak, so discouraged by life. And she, what did she need that wasn't yet to be found in Barthélémy? He was crying, his head between her tits, finger in his mouth, happy in spite of everything because she was becoming him, and anticipating his every wish, taking him right where he wanted to go: to the bathroom where he swallowed what was left of the aspirins in the bottle with a yellow label; to the living room where he played for a long time with the little monkey hanging by one arm from the palm tree; to the kitchen where the curtains had been flapping in the wind ever since the big yellow dog, making his getaway, broke the window. Oh, oh, oh, oh. Soon she would be exhausted; her arm muscles were trembling and the tips of her fingers were growing numb. She couldn't keep it up much longer. Barthélémy's weight on her neck was becoming intolerable; she was walking with her head bent too far over. She was afraid her eyes would suddenly fill up with blood and that her head would split open like an over-ripe pumpkin. Tenacious, the song made its difficult way through her throat. Oh, oh, oh. She put her lips next to Barthélémy's ear so he could hear better. She always had more trouble imitating the deep voice. The springs, the springs're shot. What she was carrying in her arms disgusted her. This false woman was repulsively ugly. She wished she were on the roof of the house so she could throw her off and be rid of her for ever. (Call the police. Have him locked up. He's gonna be the death of you. Oh, I can't go on.) At the end of the kitchen she stumbled over the carpet. Her knees popped, buckled. Sing. Sing, damn it! She was afraid. Why didn't he kill her right away since he found her unworthy of the mysteries they were performing? She made an effort to rise — her back hurt too much. And no saliva in her mouth. Wasn't it possible to rest here on the carpet, give themselves up to the tiredness which was fogging their minds, ready to help them sleep? But she musn't let go of him. She held him close. He opened his mouth and began to lick one of her tits. I'm pleased with you, Jeanne D'Arc. But undress me. Your little wife wants to be naked and right for you. She did as he asked; she laid him on the carpet, where he rolled over on his stomach so she could unzip his dress. (Fascination at the sight of the naked flesh.) Could a woman's back be so hairy? She opened the dress wider, unfastened the brassière and carefully caressed Barthélémy. It was as if she were giving him a rubdown, her hand went round and round, a tethered white she-goat walking in circles. When she touched Barthélémy's buttocks he groaned with pleasure and turned over. He had closed his eyes and from his parted lips came strong breath. It was all she liked about him, those powerful odors which had such an effect on her, unsettled her so. She was on all fours over him. The pants could fall now, he wouldn't notice; in Barthélémy's head the rites were taking on a troubled dimension. He was trying as hard as he could not to move. He wouldn't kick Jeanne D'Arc in the chest right away, he wouldn't gouge her eyes out yet, for he didn't know at this point that she was to blame for everything, that she alone was the lie and the ruse. For the moment he was thinking only of the pleasure he was about to have. Thus his buttocks tightened as Jeanne D'Arc nibbled his toes. This was the act by which he was going to trick her into admitting things which would compromise her forever. He wouldn't be impatient like last time and beat her too quickly. In any case, she couldn't call the cops because he'd finally thought of cutting the telephone wires. That was what had always saved her; she took advantage of the fact that he was momentarily CHA-O ... ed to get away from him and call the police. That was why, in a previous performance of the mysteries, he hadn't finished strangling her: because of the cops knocking at the door. All he'd had time to do was drag Jeanne D'Arc to the clothes closet and lock her in it. Lucky thing she hadn't screamed! It was true, though, that he'd given her a solid punch in the eye, and that the pain trying to get out, flee, flowing into the old shoes at the back of the closet, had left her without the strength to scream. (Would you believe me if I said I loved you?) She would have liked to swear it but the words wouldn't come. Her hands wandered up and down Barthélémy's thighs; she had just pulled his dress up to his waist. His prick was sticking straight up like an offering to the black gods of the night. She was enjoying herself. She didn't know why she got so much pleasure out of rubbing her large tits against the male sex. It was making her chest tingle. It especially pleased her to think that maybe Barthélémy was finally dead and that only his prick, still full of life, had kept going. She stretched out her tongue. What she was sucking was good, there was a taste of flowers in her mouth, or of candy or new leather. Meanwhile, somebody was slapping her on the back; that told her she should suck harder so Barthélémy could little by little escape from his lethargy. Barthélémy's left leg (my bad one, he thought) moved first. Then he began to tap Jeanne D'Arc's large ass with his foot. (The big yellow dog or the hippopotamus was on the bed again, he reflected.) Pull, pull on it hard as you can, my Jeanne. If he completely forgot himself, what would become of him? But his foot found Jeanne D'Arc's gaping cunt. He fell into the trap. After that everything happened rapidly, troubling scenes collided with each other in Barthélémy's head and he suddenly became like an overheated, exploding can of spraynet. (And those odors they were giving off, both of them soaked with joy and delight.) Barthélémy's body uncoiled on the carpet, shedding its slough; he became a long boa whose tail, stuck solidly in Jeanne D'Arc's cunt, would eventually wear down what within her he had never understood. She let the serpent wrap himself around her, she'd never known so much joy; raucous, rasping noises came from her throat, she was going to die blaspheming in the serpent's grip. Her cunt gurgled. Oh, to live like this forever, welded into one, tossing wildly about on the carpet, inflamed with this unsuspected love with which they were paying each other tribute after long months of shameful silence. (Only once Barthélémy's hands were firmly fixed on her throat did she understand that something was wrong, that maybe they'd gone too far.) She thought of the doll's head with no eyes that she had put in Barthélémy's overnight bag to make him angry and regretted having done it. He would never forgive her arrogance (which perpetuated everything bad from their past) and was going to make her pay with her life. She didn't even struggle as the hands grew tighter. Her legs slid slowly down Barthélémy's; contemptuously proud even as she submitted, she waited for him to stick his thumbs in her eyes and push them out through her ears. You goddamn bitch of a slut. I think I'm gonna give you a good beatin'. He spoke those words to her through his sick

56

smile. If she hadn't been so weary she would have tried to understand what lay behind that screen of words. He threw her down on the floor. The noise her elbow made striking the chair's rocker. The red flashes flying through space, destroying life, sending the world twirling downward like a deck of cards tossed into the air. (Hey, Lémy, I'm chokin'. Hey, Lémy. Hey, Lémy.) He was paying no attention to her, he was desperately searching for something stored away deep in his memory, no doubt something he could use to pry himself loose from her, to deliver himself from this presence which, to destroy him, refused to be him. He went and sat Indian-style at the other end of the kitchen, his hair matted on his damp, sweaty forehead, his eyes bulging, his tongue hanging out. He needed to believe he was an animal, some horrible creature out of a television cartoon. That would provide him with a means of revenge. He would let himself wander into the far off, forbidden reaches of massacre; it would sanctify him and his Jeanne D'Arc would become a good, soft woman who would heed his commands forever after. (She don't know what they do to you, she don't know about the needles, or about the tubes, she don't know nothin' about what comes into your head when the white guards jump on you tryin' to hurt you, nothin' about the cops, she don't know nothin' and don't wanna know nothin', she just chews her gum, mouth wide open in front of the TV an' it don't bother her if I die 'cause she don't know how to love me like I want.) He lit his big pipe hoping to find some peace. Why was Jeanne D'Arc in the middle of the kitchen on the carpet, sobbing, reminding him of the reason for all his suffering? When his pipe went out he unclenched his teeth and let it fall between his legs. He yawned. Maybe I oughta go to sleep and forget all about her; she don't even deserve a beatin'. He yawned again. (The large mouth to catch giant mosquitoes.) He was waiting for something which wouldn't come because his head hurt too bad and kept him from finding the right kind of torture. (Outside, rain was falling. The barrel under the drainpipe would be full tomorrow and the little birds would drink from the navels of the yellow pumpkins.) He brought his hands together with a clap. I've never been sick. They made it all up to hang me. Joseph-David-Barthélémy Dupuis' my name and the world belongs to me. I just gotta open my arms an' it'll come rushin' in. (In the yard the big, yellow dog, frightened by the thunder, was barking and pulling on his chain. The dog house moved a little each time he jerked his head. Soon the house would give and he would drag it with him to the back steps. In a single bound he would reach the window and put his wet paws on the ledge. Then he would yelp loudly so Barthélémy would come out and rub him between the ears. But since nobody would come he would grow angry and bang his head against the window until the glass broke. Then he would jump through the opening and be choked to death, hanging grotesquely in midair, held by his collar. The paws, Barthélémy thought. (Why the paws?) He tried to chase away this image of the dog with a swipe of his hand. Since he couldn't, he raised himself into a squat and started hopping around the kitchen. He finally collided with Jeanne D'Arc's body, and, striking it, forgot that he was supposed to go open the window. (Lémy, are we both crazy?) He needed to see her mouth; for things to continue there absolutely had to be blood on Jeanne D'Arc's lips. But he saw only spit and her tongue between her teeth. He laid his head on Jeanne D'Arc's belly, his heavy breathing causing her pubic hair to sway as he sniffed the odors of the sperm which must have been flowing slowly out of her cunt. (It's your fault if the baby's dead. He wasn't five months old and you were already feedin' him coke, goddamn it. Were you crazy, for Christ sake?) He laughed at his joke. But joking wasn't going to make it any easier now that he'd missed his chance to get rid of her quickly. He had to wait, be patient; sooner or later something would happen. The mysteries would begin again when she said or did something, maybe it was even better to wait for her to start. (That's it, I'll wear you down. You won't be able to stay there all night like a marble statue, starin' at the ceilin'. At some point it'll get to you an' then, bang, I'll help you keep your pretty little mouth shut for good!) He laughed again. He, not Jeanne D'Arc, held the long end of the stick. That made him happy, it was all that counted, this certainty that he was the absolute master of his work and that, when he was ready, he would finish it. For the moment, he was reflecting. No doubt he had just swallowed the ritual aspirins, which was why all was turbulence and confusion inside him. Suddenly into his house came a steady stream of bats and other bird-like creatures, covered with fuzz, which he'd have to identify before morning. His blood was hot in his veins, his head was boiling, his bones were going to melt, the kitchen was going to be flooded with winged creatures as he oozed. (Coo, coo, coo.) He stared in amazement as they rubbed their feathers against him. The kitchen was filling up with friendly eyes. He saw himself dressed in a thick robe, his beard so long he was walking on it. There was burning sand beneath his feet and his staff resembled a long, sun-baked snake. He was spitting, astonished to see the gobs turn into golden seeds and be devoured by enormous animals lying hidden in the earth, their maws open wide. Barthélémy punched himself hard in the ribs. They were rare now, visions which didn't frighten him, such as this one. Usually there was that business of the hippopotamus or the big dog or the life-sized doll or else those dumbfounding scenes in the butcher shop of Morial Mort Supermarket. He belched. He shouldn't have because his eyes came back uglier than before: he saw himself as he was, wrinkled and lined, nose full of blackheads, splotchy bibulous skin, yellow teeth and no woman to help him forget the fact. It continued to thunder and lightning, denying the night its peace. They would soon founder in the agony of the end, so many desires kept deep within. (Ahahahah-ahah-ah!) He began to hop, changed back into that deformed frog lost in his ludicrous croaking. As always, he'd forgotten Jeanne

D'Arc, that is, he didn't remember that he'd locked her in the clothes closet. He was sure he'd already killed her. Wasn't the big yellow dog eating her remains in the back yard? It took Barthélémy quite a while to unlatch the door. When he stepped onto the porch he inhaled deeply. There was a humid smell of early autumn with its turning leaves and rotting vegetation. The crude oil spewing out of the refineries wasn't yet falling over Morial Mort. The wind must have been carrying it into Bout-de-l'Île, to places called Pointes-aux-Trembles, Repentigny, Champlain, Saint-Sulpice and Lavaltrie. Going down the steps, Barthélémy took care they didn't creak. He didn't want to alert the dog, who was busy with his leftovers. (Don't start barkin', you bastard, don't start barkin'. It's old Barthélémy comin'.) Lying in front of his house with a piece of meat in his mouth, the big dog watched as Barthélémy came towards him. Then he began to growl, feeling threatened by the man's presence. Down, down boy, it's old Barthélémy. The first bark cut cleanly through the night's denseness. Barthélémy whistled. (Not a word out of you, you crazy fucker. It's simple. All I want's a little bone.) But what if the dog had eaten so much of Jeanne D'Arc that he now had her surliness within him? It wasn't going to be easy to soften him up. For how could you oblige a man who had just tossed you Jeanne D'Arc to eat? Don't be stupid, dog, it's me, old Joseph-David-Barthélémy Dupuis. The dog watched him while continuing to sniff the bones and chunks of meat between his paws. The noise of the chain striking stones changed the whole tenor of the night: there was latent violence in the air which was only waiting for something to trigger it to come tearing into Barthélémy's legs. Easy, dog, easy. Barthélémy didn't dare go any farther. The very rustling of the leaves was different, the direction of the wind had brutally changed. In his big nose was the smell of corrupt fuel oil come to deflower the virgin mist. Barthélémy took another step or two forward. Too bad for you, old dog, but I gotta have my bone too. Here I come. Watch me. He was going to have to move quickly and make some precise calculations concerning range and distance; otherwise the dog would take his hand off. He began by beating hard on the bone with a stick; the big dog jumped on it and he couldn't make him let go. He lost his stick; dozens of splinters had sunk into his palms. Now the dog was barking incessantly. All Morial Mort must have been awake and furious, all Morial Mort was going to leap as one man out of bed and grab the telephone and call the police, who were dead to the world in their little sound-proof office down at city hall. Oh, no you don't, bastard! Damn if you'll get me that way! Barthélémy wiped the sweat that was running down his forehead. Enraged, the big dog lunged, pulling his chain as far as it would go. Barthélémy took another stick and threw it on the roof of the dog house. Once again the dog leapt. You've had it now, fucker! Barthélémy jumped quickly and grabbed the bone and jumped back out of the dog's reach. Now, let's see you do that if you can, stupid! And he turned back towards the house, leaving the big yellow dog to his barking at the back of the yard. First Barthélémy had to get rid of the splinters which had gone in deep and were causing his hands to swell. He turned on the hot water, lathered his hands and waited. (Be out in no time.) He was so happy to have finally gotten the bone away from the dog he was oblivious to pain. Once the splinters were out of his hands he changed the water in the sink and added some caustic (it probably wasn't, but he liked the word for itself, for the devastating power it seemed to promise). Then he took the bone. (It's the femur, no doubt about it; nothing but a big fat thigh could cover that!) When he'd finished looking at it he dropped it in the liquid, burning his fingers. He kept his eyes on the bone, seeing in his mind naked flesh, blue veins just below the skin, a tender mass stretched between the arm chair and the table in front of the television set, measuring tape around the thigh, measuring tape forgotten when the fingers touched the down and slowly began to caress the inside of those limbs spread so wide apart.

61

(Sheer, dear flesh so near.) Barthélémy poked the bone. The bloody flesh was leaving it: soon it would be completely smooth and white and Barthélémy could then go to the bedroom. He would take the box lined with cotton wadding out of the clothes closet, put the bone in it, tie it up and crown it with a bow of pink ribbon. Everytime he killed Jeanne D'Arc Barthélémy kept one of her bones. (Because of the past, of all the things we did that were good before we got to this point.) He leaned down to put the precious box under the bed. His fingers raked up balls of dust; he blew them away. A dead spider slid across his hand. Barthélémy shuddered. Why was he shaking again? Why did he feel so terribly threatened and try to take the box out from under the bed? His hand found an old wool sock Jeanne D'Arc had left behind; it was full of dust and hair. Trying to toss the sock out of the half-open window he lost his balance and struck his head on the chest of drawers. Right away the white guards came into the room, in karate positions, each fist full of hypodermic syringes. Confused voices began to scream into the speakers and Barthélémy swung wildly about him trying to chase away the demons. It's all over, get away, in here I'm in my house, get out! I have to cry over my Jeanne D'Arc. He lay down on the floor and covered his head in his hands, trying to think only of his nose. But though it had often calmed him down in the past, this time it had no effect. So all he could do was to try to control his heartbeat. The hippopotamus was looking at him from the doorway, his large phosphorescent teeth glowing in the dark. Ah, you son of a bitch! It can't be! The police motorcycles' sirens were becoming deafening and soon the patrol car motors would be taking up every inch of des Récollets Street. Something was wrong, that was certain. Barthélémy tried to think what it could be: hadn't everything been carefully rehearsed and learnt by heart? Once Jeanne D'Arc was dead the cops weren't supposed to butt in again, Fred, Phil and Baptiste had told him he had till morning to get out of Morial Mort. (We'll be there at five a.m. and all you'll have to do is climb into Joe's old ambulance and your life'll be saved. Don't forget: five o'clock at the corner of Martial and des Récollets.) Barthélémy was so nervous all he could think about was the big yellow dog who was still barking in the back yard. At times the barks drowned out the noise of the sirens. But it wasn't sufficient, and Barthélémy knew that soon the patrol car would come screeching to a halt in front of the old parents' big house. It was no surprise when the car doors slammed. The cops stepped heavily onto the porch. Barthélémy hid under the bed, the pink-ribboned box resting on his stomach. With a little luck, if he didn't move (in spite of the white guards and the hippopotamus who had come under the bed with him) the cops probably wouldn't see him. They were coming into the house now, turning on lights and checking every room, even opening the closet doors. (It fuckin' stinks in this dump.) One of the cops sneezed. Talk about a pig! I thought the son of a bitch was still at Dorémi. I didn't think Fred was all that serious when he said we'd best come take another look before he brought Jeanne D'Arc back. If I get my hands on'im I'll rip his guts out. I'm tired of comin' here every motherfuckin' night just 'cause Jeanne D'Arc's been afraid. Why don't she get a divorce? Nobody could live their whole life with a motherfucker like that. They went into the kitchen and saw the dirty water in the sink; then they turned their attention to the red stains on the carpet. Still damp. One of the cops pressed his finger into a stain, then withdrew it and sniffed. Mercurochrome! Wanna tell me what he was doin' with that? The whole carpet's stained with mercurochrome. They went back to look attentively at the dirty water in the sink. That's a caustic solution for sure. An' that looks like flesh. Anyway, it fuckin' stinks. Yeah, it damn sure does. They walked around the kitchen some more, opened the door leading to the basement and shone their flashlights onto the stairs and into the darkness beyond. One of the cops even went down two or three steps, then stopped to shine his light methodically throughout the basement, following the beam carefully with his eyes. The other cop said, He's not in the basement, Jeanne D'Arc says he's never set foot in there again since that time we came. He's too scared. You tellin' me! come on, let's go take a look in the bedroom. OK, said the first cop, who came back up the steps and kicked the door closed. Under the bed Barthélémy made himself small, forgetting that the white guards were shooting poison into his buttocks and that the hippopotamus had raised a foot and was ready to stomp him. The cops were his real worry. His thoughts didn't travel any farther than to the feet in the doorway which he saw thanks to the flashlight's beam. Then the bedroom lights came on. Barthélémy told himself that if he didn't succeed in jumping out of the window there was no hope left for him, they'd screw him once again and everything he'd done that night would be meaningless. When the cops opened the clothes closet the doll fell into their arms. It was smeared with mercurochrome and its head, arms and legs had been cut off. I don't get this at all, one of the cops said. It's clear as day, said the other. They put the doll on the bed. Come in the kichen an' I'll explain it to you. They went away, shoe taps clicking. It's now or never, my friend. Get a move on! Barthélémy slid the box out from under the bed and then followed it, using his elbows and the small of his back. He saw one of the cops; he was squatting over a mercurochrome stain, scratching at it with his finger. The other cop must have been in front of the sink looking for the bone under the water. Barthélémy stood up. He was about to jump out the window when he dropped the box. What's that? asked one of the cops. He shined his flashlight down the corridor and straight into Barthélémy's face. Barthélémy had picked up the box, and now threw himself at the window. The pane shattered. I've got it! I've got it! I'm saved! In his excitement Barthélémy didn't notice that his forward progress had been stopped by a cop's hand around his ankle. (Whoa! Not so fast, mister!) Barthélémy held on with both hands to the window sill. He yanked and pulled hard with his leg but couldn't get free. When another hand seized his calf he let go of the sill and let himself be dragged back inside. The shattering glass had cut him around the face and arms. He was bleeding a lot but this time he had kept the box; that reassured him. The cops made him sit on the bed next to the damaged doll. They were looking so hard at the blood pouring out of his nose that they didn't see at first the box he was hiding in his lap beneath his arms. (What's that?) Barthélémy didn't answer. He sat quietly holding the box. The cop put out a hand, palm up. You'd be better off giving it to us right now, that'd simplify things. Barthélémy shook his head no. The cop who had stuck out his hand raised it above his head. The hard slap knocked Barthélémy back on the bed; he curled up in a knot to protect the box. (Hand it over, asshole!) The cops took him by the underarms, lifted him up to their shoulders and dropped him on the floor. How could Barthélémy have held on to the box? His hands released their grip and the box slid across the floor. A present for your girl friend? said one of the cops, leaning over to pick up the box. Barthélémy struggled as the other cop held him down. Take it easy, little fucker. Come on, take it easy. He couldn't let the cops open the box! They didn't have the right to play with his life that way. Barthélémy was scratching with his nails and had his mouth wide open, trying to bite the cop's leg; he was fighting with fists and legs and head. Help me here a minute, said the cop. The little bastard's a regular bearcat. The cop holding the box drew back his foot. He drove it into Barthélémy's stomach. You don't do things halfway, do you? Barthélémy's heart banged against his chest and blood spurted from his mouth. Now, maybe you'll lay still, eh? We wanna see your girl's gift too. The cop slipped a finger under the pink ribbon and lifted the top off the box. The bone was at the center, wrapped in cotton. I just don't get it, said the cop. I'll explain it all to you, said the other. You got sawdust for brains, that's why you don't get it. He put his mouth to his partner's ear and whispered. The cops laughed. Seeing the

65

bone in the cop's hand, Barthélémy forgot the pain in his stomach and the blood flowing down his chin. He lunged and took the bone out of the cop's hand and dived head first for the window. (Hey, you son of a bitch!) The cop used a foot to jam Barthélémy's leg against the wall. The other cop reached over with both arms. Barthélémy felt his hair being pulled from behind. Then they beat him till he was unconscious and left him lying on the floor. (We gonna take him in?) The voice came cracked and distorted into Barthélémy's ear. You think so? said the other. We're gonna let the fucker rot right where he is. We'll say we came and didn't find anything except the dog barkin'. The cop spit on the floor between Barthélémy's legs. We scared him enough so that when he wakes up he's gonna haul ass away from here. An' look at him, he ain't in no shape to cause trouble. And Jeanne D'Arc with Freddy. He'll take care of her. All Freddy told us to do was to give him a bad scare. Come on. The cop holding the bone had another question. And the bone? (The cops' laughter.) What d'you want us to do with that? Tomorrow we give our report to the judge an' warn Freddy an' then Jeanne D'Arc's gonna have 'im put away for good. The cops took a step or two, then stopped. Is it true Jeanne D'Arc sucks like a champ? That's Freddy talkin', not me. I personally don't like to have it nibbled. I just like to put it in nice an' easy where it's supposed to go. Well, let's split. Before turning out the lights and leaving the bedroom, the two cops had bent over Barthélémy. One of them had reached and felt his heart. He's solid. He won't die. Contemptuously, they crossed his hands on his chest, and just as contemptuously wrapped his fingers around the bone and placed a pillow under his head. They sneered. Barthélémy had heard nothing, and yet the two cops' words and mocking laughter, the things they had done to him he would somehow remember, it would all surface one day bringing intense, burning hatred in its train. Before leaving the house, the cops inspected all the rooms once more. Then the hinges of the door squeaked, the blind banged against the glass panel, the patrol car's motor revved up and the tires left two long black streaks on the asphalt. For a long time in the dark room Barthélémy's body lay, drifting towards the valley of bones where he would create a Jeanne D'Arc according to the picture of her he carried within him. Joseph-David-Barthélémy Dupuis had been badly beaten: large chunks of dried blood deformed his cheeks and webbed and matted his hair. His nose was swelling and the anger in his stomach carried nauseating gases. But why was he journeying through the long night with a smile? Was it because once, long ago, resist was the last word he had heard? In that case, it mattered little to remember who had uttered it since the fog was already lifting its siege above the Rivière des Prairies. In the yard, no bone to gnaw, the big yellow dog howled and howled −))

CUT SIX

((Hey, what's happenin' to me? Barthélémy wondered, coming to. He was walking in darkness, trying to figure out why his leg was hurting so much all of a sudden, and when he stepped on a hand a bloodcurdling scream shook the kitchen. Barthélémy reeled backwards. His head struck the wall, at least he thought so as he fell. Something was clutching him, tearing him to pieces, he was being crushed in the hippopotamus' maw, which was so vast he felt like a tiny particle of food clinging to a tooth. He tried to get away, moving hurriedly along the wall on all fours. Outside, the big dog was growling, it was still storming, the house was booby-trapped, calamities abounded, there was fire in his lungs. (Had he never left Dorémi and was he reliving one of those nights past?) He was out of breath but he didn't slow up. The stinging blows of the switch on his buttocks, they were what really hurt. A hand came down hard on his leg, then grabbed his ankle. He collapsed with a shudder and began to roll on the dusty, filth-encrusted floor, twisted with fear, slobbering and crying, piss all over his stomach and between his legs. (Jeanne D'Arc, my Jeanne, my Jeanne!) So, that was what he was afraid of then, Jeanne D'Arc's hand twisting his ankle? What he was learning about himself amazed him and scared him. Would he always have to resort to tricks to carry out his violence? In his head he saw sorts of big, black scarecrows beating their arms. Anger of a kind he had never felt before was rising up in him. He'd wanted everything to come from him alone, wanted Jeanne D'Arc's murder to be his creation, to come entirely out of his head, without artifice and without provocation, in the purity of his hatred and from the very heart of his insanity. Now it wouldn't happen that way since Jeanne D'Arc, in a single act, had destroyed his world and its threats. (Lémy, why don't you tell me you love me?) He had remained in the position in which Jeanne D'Arc had caught him; he had become the old dog stuffed with straw in the old parents' living room. Lémy, if you keep laughin' at me you'll see what'll happen. Tell me, little woman, tell your mister an' let's see. I'm tired of bein' your slave and livin' a dog's life while you play the big shot an' stay drunk all the time too. I wanted a husband, not a lousy drunkard. You can't even get it up. You'd think you had a pig's tail down there, it's all corkscrew-like. He listened calmly to the rest as he thought of the film he had seen on television. (The two armies lined up facing each other on the vast plain. The harnessed horses pawing the earth. The helmeted knights joking. The pennants flapping hard in the wind — and thus in the kitchen someone had dug up the buried, rusty hatchet. And that person was going to die. I'm gonna ram a fence picket up her ass an' stick her on the roof an' roast her in the sun.) He had to restrain himself: his hand curled into a fist and he came close to driving it into Jeanne D'Arc's face. Go right ahead with your talkin'. I'm gonna find another man, Lémy. That's just what I'm gonna do. I'm gonna dress up nice and take off. You don't see how beautiful I am and how good I am to you. Shut up, fuck! It's too late, Lémy. You've missed the boat. You've lost me. So cry now. How could he have restrained himself any longer? His hand opened, went high in the air and came down hard on her jaw. The noise of the blow made him think her jaw had exploded, pieces of bone sailing across the kitchen. (You rotten bastard, you dirty rotten bastard!) She was laughing and crying at the same time and he found her hideous. But wasn't he saved now that he'd driven her out of him? He could stomp her now, break her bones, and rip her open if he wanted. He had chased her out of his life, she was just a bitch dog he'd beaten to death, avenging himself on

70

her for all the humiliation and shame. (I've never had nothin' in my life, goddamnit, never nothin', they've always been there to take everything away, an' you, you're gonna pay for the whole bunch of 'em.) She was whispering now, holding her face in her hands, hysterical and ugly. Barthélémy moved away from her, reached and pulled open the refrigerator drawer. He was looking for the leather strap, the instrument of the sacrifice. He spit on it several times and carefully rubbed the saliva into the worn leather. I told you already, Lémy, I'm gonna leave if you ever beat me again. He laughed harshly to himself as he sat holding the strap on his knees. Damn if you're not a fool, my Jeanne. D'you really think that after all that's gonna happen to you, you're gonna be in any shape to leave? When I get finished with you, you're gonna be a grease spot on the rug. An' then I'll be able to pay attention to my own life. He stood up, spread his legs and stuck out his chest. He was naked, outside the wind was blowing, his prick was as hard as iron, water was running down the side of the barrel onto the porch, and something he had waited too long for was finally about to happen. He checked the strap to make sure it was solid, then slapped it against his thigh. Everything's just fine, lady. Your papa's comin' to rid you of your demons an' to punish you for your evil ways. He was standing over her, she was looking at him, rooted to the spot, struck dumb with fear. Too much blood was rushing into her head, her body was swept up in a wash of terror as she regarded the death between Barthélémy's widespread legs. She tried to scream, she told herself she should get to the telephone before it was too late; she could already hear the police motorcycles roaring to her rescue. Barthélémy was stroking his testicles, he was happy because she was afraid of him at last, she understood that he was going to kill her. It seemed to him the best way to start getting his revenge was to piss all over Jeanne D'Arc. She didn't even move when the urine landed. Her mouth tightened a little, her teeth touching, she lowered her eyes; that was all. If she didn't move maybe Barthélémy would stop there and be content with this sacrilege. The first blow of the strap hit her between the tits, taking her by surprise in her anguish. She buckled beneath the fiery lash, screaming despite her jaw. There was only one idea in her mind: get away from Barthélémy, escape, run, not to look back, not to spend the rest of her life crying. The second blow of the strap hit her in the eyes. The lights went out; it seemed to her that her left eye was hanging down beside her nose and that her blood, a thick black mass, was running down her chin. She turned over on her stomach, drawing her legs up under her, her hands over her head. Her big ass was tempting to Barthélémy, as he whipped her as hard as he could. The leather strap was like the continuation of his body, full of hatred, full of bitter hatred. (Ah, you demon, ah, you female demon!) And what could she say other than Lémy, Lémy, oh Lémy? Her muscles collapsed, hellfire seared her, licking at her enormous ass, opening up her cunt just as if Barthélémy had stuck his two fists in her up to her guts – (Turning her inside out.) Oh Lémy, oh Lémy, oh Lémy! She'd never loved him as much as at that moment, a sea of tenderness flowed through her, she was becoming insane with desire, she would have liked him to forget Fred and the long nights she'd spent with him in the black Buick parked somewhere along a deserted road. But he stood over her still, whipping her without stopping, saying, you'll soon be more holy than righteous, bitch! Oh Lémy, oh, oh! She had an orgasm which sent her spiraling to the depths of her own beauty and sailing back. It was as though she were swelling inside, she couldn't stop herself, she began to piss, panting in heat, itching, squirming. The odors spewing out of her cunt were driving Barthélémy crazy with rage. The strap like fireworks, a wheel of light and their wild love's ultimate weapon. I love you, Lémy, oh, oh, oh, I love you so much. Now he was kicking her again and again in the ribs. Her body would rise off the floor and he would catch it in midair with his foot, needing desperately to hurt his Jeanne D'Arc, break her in two. She hadn't been able to wait for him, she hadn't known how to satisfy a single one of his desires. (At what moment did she understand that he was really going to kill her?) She leapt between his legs towards the door she was already opening in her mind. Barthélémy flailed away; the blows of the strap were breaking her bones. She was vulnerable now that she had dropped her guard, and Barthélémy's foot went into her stomach as though it were butter; and the tits were too tempting, they were such an easy target. Every blow sent her sprawling, she would get up only to be knocked down again, moving round and round in the aura of Barthélémy's strap, trapped in circular flight, covered with blood, obsessed with the vision of the door she wouldn't have time to reach to get away from Barthélémy. (The cops had loosened their shirt collars. Ensconced in their padded chairs, they were playing cards and drinking steaming coffee from plastic cups. They weren't going to come defend her, they weren't going to come free her again from Barthélémy's clutches; they were going to let her be killed; all they cared about were the quarters that were pocketed each time a side won a game. They were laughing too hard to hear the telephone should it ring; they didn't even know Barthélémy was back and terrorizing Morial Mort. And, then, it was pouring rain, to go out in the storm when it was so nice inside just didn't make any sense.) I can't take it Lémy. I can't take it. She was dragging herself across the floor, and her body — that must have been what a swelling tumor looked like. And blood spurting everywhere as Barthélémy ripped her to shreds. (And above all: her cunt like a hanging clump of smelly entrails.) I told you I'd kill you! Go to hell, let the devil take you! It was that rage; she was powerless against it, left battered and wallowing in her own scalding-hot blood. She was plummeting downward in the void, she was a tiny, tiny bird too weak to stay in the sky. The blows kept coming, hacking her to pieces, crushing her skull. (Oh, how much longer before the motorcycles would come, the sirens be

73

heard? Would he have time to finish his work or would they surprise him stuffing her cunt with rags soaked in gasoline?) He let the strap fall to the floor: there was no danger of his violence diminishing; from within his despair he could pound and pound the rest of his life because he had been too patient too long, because he had suffered so much from being alone, so terribly alone with her. I told you, goddamn it! I told you! He didn't realize that he had picked up the strap and had begun to whip her again. (Take that, bitch! Take it, take it, take it!) And in spite of it all he had never been so calm. He was thinking that it wasn't him who was kicking and beating her but, instead, something like his anger itself that was doing it, whose shape he could almost make out. In fact, he himself was seated on the refrigerator watching through the clouds of smoke coming out of his pipe this show that was being put on by two actors saddled with roles that were too much for them. He was watching the massacre with indifference. And anyway, he'd never loved Jeanne D'Arc. Too much of a cock teaser for my taste. How're you supposed to live with somebody who's always tryin' to cross you, trick you, always lyin' to you? An' a one track mind, too. Fuckin', nothin' but fuckin'. An' TV. An' too lazy to have little mongoloids. A real idiot. An' Jeanne D'Arc you're lucky your Barthélémy don't know nothin' about the Caisse Populaire manager an' his big car comin' to a halt in a cloud of dust. Poor old Barthélémy, he still don't know that they were layin' down on the seat, Jeanne D'Arc an' the manager, eatin' each other out. I'm itchin' to see Barthélémy an' Jeanne D'Arc too when he finds out about that! He was laughing, satisfied with his own role which was to plant suspicion in Barthélémy's mind in order to feed his bad faith and the disgust he felt for Jeanne D'Arc and see them grow fast. (Here, take that, bitch! Take that!) She didn't even try to get out of the way of the blows. The only thing in her mind was to get to the door and roll down the steps so the cops would see her and recognize her. (Stuffed doll being chopped in little

74

pieces.) She saw herself in the butcher shop, Big Fat Seguin was sharpening his knives, the hoisting gear was ready. Two men were holding her by the ears as Big Fat Seguin felt for the jugular vein. When he found it he would slice the flesh with his knife and blood would run all over his hands, she would let out a horrifying scream and her mouth would fill up with sawdust. Then her head would empty, nothing more would happen, her brain would stop functioning, she'd vaguely realize that they were turning her over on her back the better to watch her die. And her cunt like a fish's mouth, opening, closing, blowing bubbles. After that a veil would fall over everything, death's own shroud, there in the cold in the transparent cellophane bag. And thus why would she cry when Big Fat Seguin disemboweled her, taking out the heart, the stomach, the liver? She would never hear music more beautiful than that of the saw cutting through her thorax. And after that she would really die, that is, everything would begin to get small: there would be concentrations of energy, the bodies would become one hundred watt bulbs with gnarled feet, the bodies would shine so brightly they'd sear her eyes, turning them to charred stone. And as all got smaller all would be spinning wildly in a world growing colder and colder. She would be a snowflake, she would fall heavy and maternal from the sky, she would fall for Barth-élémy who had already been waiting too long, who was going mad sitting Indian-style and alone in the kitchen with grandfather's old pipe between his teeth, talking, words stumbling over each other in his mouth to finally form obscure sentences sprung from his delirium, his fear, the anguish he felt at being abandoned and too naked and too ugly without Jeanne D'Arc who had found bliss now that the hook was ready and she was bound hand and foot, now that there were straps round her wrists and ankles and she was awaiting her assumption, eventually to reside among the sides of beef and the pigs ticketed by the Federal Government. Only to come back to earth when Big Fat Seguin stuck the four tragic bottles of beer in her. Whatever pride she had left would be awakened but she would be unable to get free of her bindings, and exhaustion would take hold of her and turn her upside down, grab her head and twist and shake it roughly, walk all over her body, even stick a carrot in her ass and an enormous leek stalk up her cunt. She would tumble downward head over heels, downward, downward for days, she would tumble downward head over heels for days. Her body: Ste Catherine's taffy-elastic bubblegum on the bottom of a shoe. (Oh, I love you so much, my Lémy. Forgive me!) But how, there at the extreme limit of his violence, how could he have listened to her? Didn't she know he put cotton in his ears when he beat her? Couldn't she see he had had it, that he was beating her so desperately and so savagely because he couldn't stand having yielded to the provocation she'd maliciously wrapped herself in? And he had no choice, he had to continue hurting her: there was so much pent up anger in his feet and fists that he thought the sacrifice could never end, thinking rather that he was going to go on with it, and on and on with it, conjuring it anew. Was that all she could do, Jeanne D'Arc – change before his eyes into a rotting beast from which sooner or later he'd have to think of freeing himself? (Her eyes, her feet, her tits, her pulpy buttocks, her belly and loins, the magnificent roundness of both belly and loins, with the altar in the shadowy hollow protected by the mountains of flesh that were her thighs – now mutilated and burned by the red-hot ashes from the pipe he'd emptied on her knees.) Lémy, Lémy, Lémy! Forgive me, Lémy! You're nothin' but a cheap, painted whore! He was crying, his eyes wandering in the void; the strap was raised, ready to strike Jeanne D'Arc's body. He was suffering terribly. I really would have liked for things to happen otherwise, an' instead of beatin' you – (no). He couldn't soften up when everything was just beginning; he couldn't let himself think or speak. He'd do that later once the morning, in the whiteness of its dawn, allowed the error to come to an end. He would be barefoot and bloody, he would walk behind the house in the cold dew; he would go near the pumpkin patch, there where the big yellow dog was tied up, and with his back against the side of the dog house and the animal's head on his knees he would explain everything, all that had happened that night, how he had bathed himself beneath Jeanne D'Arc's body in the blood running out of the thousand wounds made by the butcher knife stolen from Morial Mort Supermarket. He grabbed Jeanne D'Arc by the legs and began to pull her around the kitchen. (I'm even better than a team of horses. I can haul a load of wood all by myself.) On he trudged, snorting, avoiding stumps, stepping over low-hanging branches, climbing hills. (There's nobody can beat me when I really get goin'. I can do in a day what nobody else in this world could.) He was dragging his load of wood roughly along behind him, paying no attention whatsoever to it. Let Jeanne D'Arc complain, let her yell and weep, it wasn't going to help her any. The horse knew what he was doing, that was all that was important. So he let him take his own course throughout the kitchen. Jeanne D'Arc's body banged into the furniture, her head was a pile-driver splitting the floor, (Oh, I'm done for, I'm really done for this time.) He kicked her in the jaw, jumped on her with both feet, caving in her ribs and crushing her kidneys. Then she was still, her bulging eyes staring at the light bulb shining down round and white out of the high, heavy shadows. Barthélémy wasn't even looking at Jeanne D'Arc at this point, he was too tired and knew that he wouldn't be able to finish what he had started, he hadn't the strength, would never have, every time it would be the same thing. He was pulling her even more roughly now. If only his madness could come back! He'd have welcomed it with open arms because he was fed up with this business that was robbing him of his night and of the dreams he'd had when they were first together, happy and complacent both of them. He must have swallowed another whole bottle of aspirin and drunk two Pepsis before finding the courage to go down to the basement. He was hopping like a toad, holding a lighted match in front of him, looking for a saw. The cockroaches fled the light, and no doubt it was rats moving between the cases of empty bottles. Entering the basement, the noises from outside became a thousand times more evocative and were so loud they left him dazed. Barthélémy thought he'd become a gigantic ear. His legs gave out. His hands were too small to cover the Ear. Packing cases were riding his back, tools tumbled down on him, and a pair of shiny pruning shears stuck in the dirt, trapping his neck. Barthélémy stuck out his tongue, swallowed sawdust, then spit. His bare feet became a ground hog's paws scratching into the earth. The noise caused his organs to burst, his lungs came out of his mouth and stained the wall in front of him. (Christ, I gotta get outta here!) His eyes were burning, his heart was skipping beats and about to stop, he was dying again as he scratched away at the black earth; demons were swallowing his prick, sucking it, biting it. He was struggling so much, attacked by the old horrifying visions, that his tired muscles tore as he screamed. The basement was filling up with white guards who were pushing the terrible hippopotamus in front of them, the beams became enormous hypodermic needles coming at his buttocks to paralyze him for life; and then the badges of the cops, hanging by their hands from the beams, finished him off, he sank like a stone into the cold, familiar nightmare, shoulders cut by the cable with which he was pulling the toboggan where worms were wriggling happily, full of Jeanne D'Arc's life. In the basement the world was receding, partitions were collapsing, the jars of nails and screws lined up on the workbench were falling, in the drain-pipes troubled water was backing up, rising. Muttering incoherently, he was wading in excrement as he looked for the saw, and the cop motorcycles turning round and round in his head forced him to his knees in all the mess. I'm gonna die! I'm gonna die! The only act he was capable of now was screaming those words over and over, but they promised no reprieve, everything was splitting and cracking, everything stunk, everything was emptying like an open intestine. (The sirens! Those goddamn sirens! Those goddamn sirens!) He put a hand to his forehead, blood was trickling down his face, the white guards were quartering him, the cans of gasoline were being emptied: the match was struck against the side of the box, he burst into flames, a human torch rolling in the dirt and dust. The sound of pots and pans falling, of bottles breaking against the walls, the sound of intense pain boring through his burning prick.) He screamed, mama, mama, oh mama, oh mama! Then he threw himself head first through the basement window; shards of glass cut his face and left an eyeball hanging down his cheek. In the back yard the big yellow dog stood on his hind legs, his barks penetrating the curtain of blood. (Hey you, don't you sleep at night? You tryin' to get taken in?) He lifted his head towards the threatening voices; the big cops were shining their flashlights at him. He hid his eyes, ashamed of being naked and filthy, ashamed, too, that he had just come from hell. Why don't you leave me alone. I'm waitin' for my wife, my Jeanne's not here yet. The two cops spit on the grass, they each stuck out an arm and lifted him up by the shoulders. We're gonna haul you in for disturbin' the peace, friend. He struggled but couldn't break the cops' iron grip. They dragged him over in front of the steps and set him down on a stump; they looked at him, then shined their flashlights in his eyes once again. At the end of the alley the murmur of muffled engine farts. On the roof the red bubblegum machine was a whimsical radar beam infiltrating the nooks and crannies of the night. The patrol car looked like a mutant bird grown too big to fly. You can't take me in, I ain't done nothin', OK? I had a couple of beers an' maybe made some noise. What you got against me anyway? It gets on your nerves waitin' up all night for your wife. Sit down on the steps an' I'll open three beers an' we'll slap each other on the back an' I'll tell you my story an' you tell me yours, OK? One of the cops was playing with his hat.

His damp hair lay flat against his temples. Barthélémy stared at the cop's forehead, at the red line running across it. The cop smelled of sweat. His shirt was dripping wet at the armpits, two white circles giving off a foul odor. The cop's gut was huge, like his forearms and hands. The nightstick looked curiously fragile in his grip, a vulnerable object he had to caress so it wouldn't break or start whining in the night. (Yeah, well, what you're gonna do, friend, is to get back inside that house an' turn off the lights an' go to sleep. What's all that about Jeanne D'Arc? You drink too much Joseph-David-Barthélémy Dupuis. You know Jeanne D'Arc's been dead a week. You know you weren't there when she died. They had you locked up in Dorémi because you'd been drunk as a skunk for two solid months and wanted to shoot her.) Barthélémy stuck his fingers in his ears. He didn't want to hear the lying voices any more and was trying to stop the venom from rising to his head. His eyes were full of water, the cop car's headlights refused to leave the night alone: the firmly fixed trees, the yellow leaves and scraps of paper scudding beneath the bright chrome of the automobiles parked nearby — all became suspect. Yes, flee, get away from the two cops whose hands planted on his shoulders were going to force him to sit there. My ass is killin' me. Don't you see I'm sittin' on a knot that's stickin' right in me, damn it! The cops laughed and winked at each other. Barthélémy was trembling; he had his hands around his ankles. He was frantically trying to find an idea he'd had which the cops had chased away. The big blue vein on his wrist had disappeared; it must have sunk back beneath the skin, and it would stick to the bone and cause him terrible pain the rest of his life. He pinched himself. He couldn't let his mind wander while the two cops were standing there terrorizing him. Alright, OK, I'm goin' in to bed. That what you want? The hands grew heavier on his shoulders, the fingers dug into his flesh. A hand opened before his eyes and slammed into his cheek, lifting his head off his shoulders. He could feel the shadows pulling him from behind, bloody stars shot into his eyes. (Listen, we didn't come here to fart around; we're takin' you in an' then you'll get more than taps. They'll serve you some knuckle sandwiches, got me? An' you're lucky we're givin' you that much of a chance.) He wanted to thank them for their generosity but he couldn't take his mind off his swollen cheek, his skin that was now full of blood and going to turn blue. An' I can't get up. His muscles were dead. His eyes were mere slits as he looked at the cops, tongue between his teeth, curly, matted hair making two horns, one on each side of his head. The cops must have felt provoked since one of them belched and the other muttered a threat. Then they pushed him backwards as he wrapped himself into a terrified ball; the door was opened with a foot and he was thrown into the house. The floor groaned. He heard the cops saying, I think we've scared him enough for one night. But he didn't understand. He was still in the hallway, ashamed of having acted so cowardly with them, crying as he unfolded his arms and legs. Then he shrugged his shoulders and told himself it was better not to think of anything; he was too afraid of losing himself again for nothing, winding up in the grip of an obsession, completely disoriented and unable to go anywhere his obsession didn't push him. He was sick, going to die. Like a poisonous flower gangrene would climb up his leg, destroying his muscles, darkening his skin; so they'd amputate, all he'd have left would be stumps which would move in a pitifully clumsy fashion when he was lying on his back in the white hospital bed and a guard came to have him do exercises after changing his dressing − the hospital, oh, oh, oh, the hospital! (Since you knew you were going to die why pretend you weren't?) He began to slap himself in the face. Come on, Lémy, forget all that, it's mornin', there's no more danger. He groaned with each slap, the pouch beneath his eye began to twitch, the poison in his head began to act: all was already lost: there was no longer any place, neither in his head nor in his feet nor in his chest, no place where he could be happy, where wagging your prick meant satisfaction, where to sit and smoke in peace wasn't betrayal, where thinking of Jeanne D'Arc didn't become a bear trap whose springs would send the blades down on his legs, cutting them off. Barthélémy was crying still, an old sinful image, an old solitary voice lying forgotten on the floor. He grabbed the bottles in the cupboard, he couldn't help it, the dusty bottles full of a liquid future, hot broth, tepid piss he'd down greedily, crouching on the rug. Oh, the future, the future, so much future to swallow! He belched several times, licking his lips as he stared at the wallpaper; the yellow puppies were nice to look at, they were playing with the big red ball which in an affectionate mood he had drawn on the wall to help them find the time less long. Was he about to come down with the daytime's fever, was it going to force its way through the windows and doors of the old parents' house, was he to be stricken and wrenched inside out and made forcibly a part of what was going on in the street, there where cars were raising clouds of dust, where soon children would pass, dressed in baseball uniforms, their gloves hanging off the bats on their shoulders, where the old black women returning from mass would greet each other amicably, where – where birds and paper and stones and leafy trees and earthworms and people would come together in a surge of lovely sights and sounds. Barthélémy clapped his hands – Chinese baby happy, happy, happy! He got to his feet thinking that he was a splendid rooster, haughty there in the middle of the kitchen, brilliant of crop and crest, eyes like two small suns mounted shallowly in his head. Cockadoodledoo, oh, oh cockadoodledoo! (Let'em hear some cockadoodledoos, little biddy!) He was exultant, running round in circles on the carpet flapping his wings as though he wanted to fly, his neck tensed, his majestic breast thrust out before him. He was the cock of the walk, sealed off in his grandeur and pride. Cockadoodledoo, cockadoodledoo, oh, oh, cockadoodledoo! (Yeah, fuck, I'm gonna let all of you have it with my cockadoodles!) But already his eye was dimmed, already his crest was wilting, the yellow of his spurs fading, feathers falling with each flap of his wings. The dulled, clumsy cock stumbled along, having a hard time finding the grain thrown his way, opening his beak and pecking only to come up with pebbles. Barthélémy would see him hesitate, then obstinately peck at the stone, growing enraged. Soon the cock began to stagger; his beak was cracked, his eyes stared dully from behind feather frames. Cock-owl with broken feet falling over backwards, exhausted, without – they would have been a blessing had they been rotten even – any teeth to put his tongue between. His organs told Barthélémy he was old and used up, out of whack, unable to go on with the mysteries. His strength was gone, he was too tired to even notice that he was slobbering. The saliva running down his chin made streaks in his chest hair. Had he been nailed to the wall, left this last little bit of life the better to suffer, the better to understand to what point he'd been servile and had failed to live what he might have lived? He banged his head against the wall several times. He needed no pretext now, nothing was to be hidden any longer beneath the mysteries' artifice, it was too late to play games. All was waiting to be finished and had to be done here and now before the cops got back. That was what Jeanne D'Arc's loud moans at the other end of the kitchen made him suddenly understand. He stood up to listen better, then spit blood which was coming out of his wounded gums, then walked down the hall, arriving thus in front of the basement door. Then it hit him. Yeah, that's right, I gotta go to the basement and get the saw, he thought –))

CUT SEVEN

((However, it took him a while to convince himself that he really had no choice, that once again he had to go downstairs. He finally opened the door and put his foot on the top step. He was bent over because his kidneys hurt. There was a tight knot of pain in in the small of his back, which surprised him because he didn't remember the cops kicking him there before throwing him as hard as they could into the house. But they're gonna come back an' do it, so it amounts to the same thing. He groped around in the dark. At last he found the flashlight and when he pushed the button a stream of weak yellow light pierced the darkness. Now he could go down to the basement, no one would attack him as long as the batteries held out. He searched methodically for the saw, combing the dark corners, the mildewed cardboard boxes, the enormous crocks, the chests. He put the jars of nails back in their places, gathered up the screws which had fallen off the workbench, turned the handle so the two sides of the vise would touch, and rebuilt the pyramid of maple logs beneath the staircase. But by moments a subtle fear made itself felt in him and he would think he saw shadows gliding through the darkness towards him, terribly threatening in their discretion. Then he would jump back on the stairs, crying out, his flashlight's beam sweeping across the gloom. (I think you're crackin' up, you son of a bitch. There's nobody down here, you can see that for yourself.) The saw was quickly receding from his consciousness, becoming a kind of bomb stowed away in his brain. He knew the dynamite was there and that sooner or later he'd use it, but for the moment something more urgent seemed to be calling him. He needed to look at and fondle the greasy, rusted bolts, the quart jars of nails, the cans of turpentine, and those cans of paint stolen from the docks when he and his buddies, Phil, Fred and Baptiste, were involved in the black market. In those days the basement was warm and friendly, a closed world, a gathering place for brothers. Sitting on crates, they drank home brew and smoked big cigars and told one another stories; they kidded Jeanne D'Arc who, among those rock-solid brutal men, was obsessing in her fragility. (She handled the money, using an old school bag. Just above her head was a light bulb, and her long hair flowed down the sides of her face when she leaned over the small black notebook to enter her share in large numerals. The rest of the time she sat quietly with a smile on her face, or chewed gum and winked now at one now at another merely so they'd notice her nice figure and know that her presence gave them an importance they wouldn't otherwise have had.) The shadows on the wall were reassuring, and by drinking they soon reached a state of perfect contentment. The voices were signs of recognition, extraordinarily slender threads with which they weaved everlasting unity into the world. It was unimportant what was said; the sound alone mattered — roars, laughter, farts, belches, lips smacking, the sonority of nails, the sucking noise of a dental plate quickly lifted up by the tip of the tongue, legs cracking, the music of screws taken from quart jars by the handfuls and let fall in small amounts. And the odor of tar and of paint and of turpentine, and of cigar and cigarette butts lying cold on the ground; the odor of leather and of glue and of mildew, and of wads of gum stuck under their seats; the odors that time brings out of a piece of furniture: heavy, strong, powerful odors. The police didn't come into basements in those days, they weren't pursuing old Barthélémy, weren't making his life miserable just because he drank too much and didn't sleep at night. They were left in peace, allowed to go about their business in subterranean tranquillity, unnoticed and un-

86

known and thus no bother to anyone; besides, around them, inside them, were peaceful, soothing words like sentries keeping all that might do harm at a distance till it grew exhausted and perished. Words were screws, nuts, words formed protective plates beneath the skull. (When Barthélémy thought of those days, of the gentleness of what they lived inside of words, he always felt the same amazement: had one bottle of beer too many been able to shift the very foundations of the structure they had built around themselves? With which rapidly-downed glass of home brew, which poke in the ribs with an elbow following, which satisfied slurp, did their everyday words become a trap? Who knew now? And had these words – (If you come any closer I'll smash this bottle over your head) – never been said?) There was no explanation contained in the sentence itself, in the arrangement of the words. What was being said was somewhere outside of the words. That hand high above their heads next to the light bulb on the ceiling where the fingers became transparent, showing the grease stains on the skin. Hey, your hand's really red, Baptiste! Those words of Jeanne D'Arc had changed everything: that voice full of complicity which went straight to the heart of his affection, that voice breaking the silence, was committing a sacrilege; censor-like, it was going to close down the show. Hey, is your hand ever red! They were drunk and all but deprived of language. They were slurring their words, their speech was heavy, thick, their words were falling ridiculously like little red and green wooden blocks between their legs. And Jeanne D'Arc, who was standing, and the big red hand feeling her tail, then moving down to her thighs, the big red hand not stopping till it was between her legs. (Is it hot enough for you?) All that had taken place in the murky light of the old twenty watt bulb screwed into the ceiling. It was very important that Barthélémy remember that scene, the hand spread in Jeanne D'Arc's crotch, and she not moving, not even chewing. The gum must have been stuck on the roof of her mouth or in a rotten tooth – It was extremely important that he remember that scene, the hand spread in the crotch, the large hand like an oily stain just above the wide-spread legs; and Jeanne D'Arc's matter-of-fact voice: You gonna move your damn hand or d'you want me to piss on it? It was those words striking his ears which had destroyed their whole past and thrown them brutally into the present. The home brew had almost come back up, crosses had patterned the air in front of his eyes, shadows had swept up Jeanne D'Arc's skirt to her crotch, soiling her buttocks and that cunt which was opening like a mouth deep within the hairs. He had lost his balance, the crates falling down under him noisily: everything reminded him of Jeanne D'Arc's sacrilegious words, those pernicious words which were going to destroy him, devour him; his sole defense against them being a greater sacrilege was some outrageous act or insult which probably wouldn't succeed in redeeming them since what had been said would remain said in all its repetitive monotony. His head struck a quart jar of nails but he was so angry he didn't have time to notice the blood pouring out of his nose. He was blinded by the pain his memory caused him, fixed as it was on that absurd event: that vision of Jeanne D'Arc pissing on a hand not his own showed him what suffering was in all its horror. Nothing more could happen, and no remission was possible. He was crawling between the crates, imagining that his lung was pierced by the bullet from the twenty-two that Jeanne D'Arc, taking careful aim, had fired at him. He was lying flat, swallowing earth in the basement to hide his shame. (The world was swelling slowly as his suffering grew. There was the almighty world-hippopotamus looking down at him from on high. Soon it would jump on him and crush him beneath the weight of its surliness. Why would he always have to die humiliated???) Barthélémy was bumping into the crates, overturning buckets of paint with his head. What might be within reach just beyond the quart jars of nails he didn't know, he was bewildered and exhausted by this night's

88

unreason; there was only the big red hand; it remained before his eyes refusing to go away, defying him. His head lay in piss, up out of the dirt came the warm smell of Jeanne D'Arc's urine. (I told you, you devil, I told you I'd piss on your hand if you didn't move it!) What hurt Barthélémy most wasn't that they all laughed when she said that, it was to realize that he was being excluded, that a hand placed on his Jeanne D'Arc's cunt meant an end to all intimacy, made his love impossible. Hadn't they just killed what within him was most noble – his feelings? (What're you doin' on the ground, my Lémy?) Still, he'd had the courage to raise his eyes in her direction, to look at her. What he saw on Jeanne D'Arc's face disgusted him. She was a liar, she was deceitful, underhanded, mean, vicious. His house of cards collapsed, from now on all would be lived in anger and hatred and silence. Words would no longer decide everything, be everything, they'd only be a pretext of sorts which would precipitate action, throw the world into the whirlwind of gratuitous violence from which one would emerge unrecognizable, mutilated, but finally ready to take life on. Barthélémy lowered his eyes. He only wanted to see those familiar scenes, that is, the hundred thousand Joseph-David-Barthélémy Dupuis of his dreams marching into the future with raised fists, frost, or rather blood, on their moustaches, necks strangled by silver chains, shit-stained scapularies of Holy Blessed Death, mutilated sexes eaten raw to screw up one's courage and strengthen the will, heads rolling under makeshift blades in underground chambers looking like nothing more than basements, dead bodies dumped in the trunks of old rusted cars, gloved policemen cautiously removing the bodies while photographers behind a metal fence were playing watch the birdy; and other familiar things, for example, killings all over Morial, young girls dragged into empty lots, then tied to posts, and long lines of men, pricks out, moving towards them, towards cunts open like flowers. And then it was old knives cutting up the bodies and then the pieces being thrown to the dogs prowling Sainte Catherine Street. Then it was massacres, broken store windows, the stores pillaged by phoney niggers, shoe polish disappearing slowly from their faces, drained off by the sweat running down their foreheads, their cheeks and chests showing large white spots. Then it was buses overturned (wheels still spinning, fire causing the tires to explode, burning the embossed leatherette seats, sending the springs flying, leaving hideous, twisted, glowing-red hulks lying in the middle of the streets), looters walking among the debris — and that long beautiful wedding gown thrown down into the mud and blood, with the mannequin's head split open by a machete, and those snipers on the roofs, those unrelenting machine gun bursts, those armed, invisible men in the doorways of houses where lying flat on their stomachs with chewed matches clenched in their teeth they awaited easy targets. And then sometimes it was screaming motorcycles and the disgusting eee-aww, eee-aww of armored cars as they rolled over the dead, spewing forth tear gas, laughing gas, paralyzing gas or simply messages recorded at Police Headquarters. Barthélémy saw all of that and more: Baptiste's large hand planted squarely in his Jeanne D'Arc's crotch, she pissing on it. He jumped up in order to free himself from the evil spell; then he drew back his leg and let Baptiste have it in his sack of marbles. He caught Jeanne D'Arc in the right eye with a fist at the same time. Only then, the night's long dead fuse dangling from his hand, did Barthélémy speak. It was a shouting match between him and Baptiste, the latter's main concern, however, being to protect his organs with his big hands. And then, her eye swelling, turning blue, Jeanne D'Arc started to moan. Barthélémy knew now that even violence wouldn't succeed in putting unity back in the basement, the reason being, no doubt, that it had come too late, after too much verbal complicity, too many word games, too many projections of themselves into the past. They had waited too long, they were worn out and would appear ridiculous whatever they did. The act simply lacked meaning. It was merely a geyser-like spew of emotion which had overwhelmed them and left them afraid. Maybe they were dreaming. Maybe none of it was really happening. Maybe it all belonged to the netherswirl of nightmare. (But how to know? The brain was a very small thing and that world they wanted to become a part of remained aloof, out of reach, unconcerned with what might have been happening with it. So there was only solitude, eternal self-recourse, the familiar litany of those monstrous scenes, the worn-out record of the two hundred year-old rebellion.) Who, then, could have blamed Barthélémy for his anger? Everything being lost from the start, argument and explanation were beside the point, they were much ado about nothing, as was the mumbling of phoney remorse: I know, I know I shouldn't have, fightin' never got a man nowhere. Darkness had come swarming into the basement the moment the fist smashed the bulb overhead and Barthélémy was feeling his way on all fours through the crates looking for Baptiste, whose curses, shouted in his high-pitched voice, sounded like the peeps of excited birds. I'm gonna kick your fuckin' ass, you goddamn son of a bitch. He was right beside him, with a single leap he could be on top of Baptiste and pounding away. He could never stop fighting precisely because of the guilt rising within him, the whirling currents of his cowardice which threatened to swamp him: if he didn't kill Baptiste he wouldn't have the courage to even leave the basement. But Jeanne D'Arc and other Baptistes had him by the arms and legs trying to subdue him. Barthélémy was now possessed of elemental strength, he had become a concentration of forces which had been pressed by the basement's gloom into his mouth because he'd kept it open too long. He had no choice: he had to fight: pound; punch; stomp. Baptiste's face was a bloody pulp. Worse, it was an affront, an insult to the past. Barthélémy struck with such fury hoping to free himself from all the things in his mind which had never been really possible. If he succeeded, he was certain that then even the big red hand, which had come to rest squarely in Jeanne D'Arc's crotch, would sink quickly out of sight in the abyss of that which didn't concern his life. His knuckles were sore, his fingers were digging into the flesh; Baptiste had stopped yelling a while ago, he was dead. But there was no stopping as long as Baptiste's hand remained intact. (Then he heard the jarring noise of the cops' motorcycles for the first time, and for the first time saw the fat-bellied cops spitting on the grass and dragging him by the feet on the sidewalk before beating him savagely on the legs with their long night sticks. Tongues of flame lapped at him, pouches formed and began to swell under his eyes, the pain twisted his head out of shape, letting in a whole host of new phantasms. He was gasping for breath, the lights of the night were causing explosions beneath his skull. All was lost, expecially the comforting stability of before. The world of the basement had suddenly emptied, and he, by the fact of his tranquillity, knew release. From now on he would have to live in the daytime, under the mauve lights of the cell, bereft of old habits. Jeanne D'Arc would change independently of him, always at that moment, relived a thousand times, when the big red hand came to rest between her legs. That being the case, how could he resist beating his old pal Baptiste even more viciously? The future – Yes, the future remained closed till excess should run its course. One day he wouldn't be able to go on because he'd have used up everything necessary for the future. The future, the future, the future. Abyss. Pus. Howls. Saws cutting leg bones. Stumps, stumps, stumps, stumps for the future, and atrocious fear knotting the guts, making of the heart a warm potato with long yellow sprouts growing out of the eyes, the ears, the mouth, the navel, the prick and the asshole. The future contracting, or tossed like a ball into the black void. Black, black, black. The future after too many wars, too many pitched battles, too many cops barging into peaceful basements, too many – Yes, too many fishy stories; and desire deep in his bones, and crawling without hope on his runny stumps, and the future — too much, too much, definitely too much past unlived to be able to continue, for the future to rise over one and over the wheat rotting in abandoned barns — future, future, future!) Even the fact of looking for the handsaw in the debris of the once-alive world of the basement was no more than a speeding up of the present, an illusory inflating of history. (Where the goddamn hell can it be!) He was growing impatient, cursing, terrified by the idea of the flashlight going out and plunging him into darkness and thus into a past which could only be intolerable for having been lived too many times. He was trembling uncontrollably, moving hastily throughout the basement, furious: everything was upside down, out of place, covered with dust, hostile, wrong. (My goddamn handsaw, where the hell can it be!) He opened the old pantry doors, out fell newspapers, rags, cans of paint, the derby, the two large thighbones of his brother Malcomm's beloved trotter which had been willed to him, the ribbons, the bouquet of artificial flowers worn by Jeanne D'Arc for their wedding. The handsaw had to be somewhere in all that junk, maybe on the third shelf with the hacksaw. He cut his fingers on the hacksaw and cursed. The blood he was sucking tasted like musty paper. Hey, the hacksaw, it's perfect for what I wanna do. He picked up the derby and placed it on his head. What he was about to do couldn't be done naked. It had to have an aura of ritual about it, even if it was sham. When he had pushed his hair beneath the hat, he felt reassured. (Without a doubt the derby was a means of preventing vengeance from becoming merely gratuitous violence.) Barthélémy was strolling in the basement with one hand holding the hat and the other closed tightly on the saw. He needed to convince himself he wouldn't weaken, even if the event was taking on a meaning which had escaped him till now. Things just weren't that simple: once he'd marched back upstairs and seen Jeanne D'Arc's motionless body, would he be strong enough to go through with it, to saw into that skin and make real his horrible imaginings? He was mumbling incoherently, hoping to provoke himself into action, force the profound act of this first birth which would simultaneously make all things possible and be their realization. Time was nudging him forward; there were few hours left to live before dawn. Once the sun had come in the window, its rays annihilating his flashlight's beam, piercing his ears as he stood in the shadows, it would be too late, Barthélémy would have waited too long, his act gone uncommitted. The derby grew tighter on his head while his heart, old Barthélémy's heart, beat hard. Why had it taken him so many nights to understand that new blood swelled his veins, that a river of evil forces was overrunning its banks within him? His courage was returning, accompanied by fierce, forgotten anger. He slammed the pantry doors and the noise made him even more furious. How could he not think of Jeanne D'Arc's betrayal, how could he keep all those images of her out of his head? She had never accepted the idea that she was pregnant, that the baby would come soon, that he would be ugly and covered with blood. No, no, no! I don't want to have it. He's got no legs, an' there's not a hair on his head! No, no, no! She'd never wanted to seek beyond her refusal, she'd never again spread her legs for Barthélémy; she'd killed the baby, she'd pushed it off the bed, she'd held it by the ankles and beat its head against the walls, happy to see blood coming from the wounds, happy because the crushed bones abolished her maternity. The small white coffin gliding slowly down the aisle looked like a tool box, a piece of mockery come out of Jeanne D'Arc's legs to destroy Morial Mort. Nothin' was the same after that. As far as her life was concerned, I was nowhere. He suddenly remembered that time he'd stayed in the rocking chair all day, sweating, suffering because of his leg, biting his nails without saying a word. The smell of sausages frying in beer had made him realize he hadn't eaten yet that day. A little while later Jeanne D'Arc had arrived carrying the tray chest high, her hair falling down on her shoulders, barefoot and beautiful,

beautiful tits, beautiful ass, beautiful face, beautiful womb from out of whose secret exit too many awaited children had come prematurely. She had stopped in front of him, lowering her arms so he could see the plate full of sausages and the mountains of fried onions and the potato drowned in a sea of sauce. What had she said? He was crying because she had treated him with contempt ever since his leg had forced him to stay in the rocking chair all the time: she didn't understand how unhappy his infirmity made him, and didn't see the subtle provocation in her behavior. Maybe she'd screamed at him and had picked up a sausage with the fork and said, as she put it to his lips, Come on, open your trap, you bastard, swallow it, feed your face, swallow it, swallow it! He could see her now, she was bent over him, her eyes were bulging and she was yelling so loud she was spitting in his face. But her tit was warm against his arm and filled him with joy that he could only hide by keeping his mouth closed despite the pressure of Jeanne D'Arc's hand as she tried to force him to swallow the greasy, dripping sausage. (Was that the time he'd punched her in the eye and seen her ass and the deep crack between the large folds of flesh when she fell?) Now I'm gonna give *you* a sausage to eat, you whorish bitch! He hadn't been able to get it in her hole, the sausage had fallen apart, grease had spurted out of one end. And he'd let it drip in her pubic hair as she lay unconscious beneath him. He could wait till she came to; being forced to stay off his feet for so long, he'd learned patience. He rocked slowly, his eyes fixed on the bandages which swelled his foot, thinking about the cops busting into the basement yelling and swinging their clubs. The first blow was to his ankle and had caused him to let go of Baptiste and to curl up in a ball to hide from the cop. The blows kept landing until, finally, he played dead. But the cop wouldn't stop – Oh, that fat, dirty hippopotamus whose muzzle, whose horns, whose stamping hooves were breaking him in pieces. When they made him get up he'd screamed because of his broken ankle and the bones in his foot which the cop had crushed beneath his shoes. Goddamn! Goddamn! He'd lost his head, driven crazy by the pain that was climbing his leg and forming a knot as big as a fist in the pit of his stomach. Blinded by anger, he jumped on the cop, kneeing, punching, biting, screaming, scratching, a wounded beast, a bloody bull, drowning in his own desperation, all but finished, as the prick dangling out of his pants, shrivelled as an old carrot, showed – and the powerful punch that snapped Barthélémy's head back. Everything spun wildly like a top, flames glittering in the dark like precious stones, and sperm streaming down Baptiste's thighs as he headed for the pass leading into the black, wet, throbbing cunt at the very center of Jeanne D'Arc. Noooooooooooooooo-ooo! Barthélémy was choking, his eyes full of tears, his body like a wound or merely something shameful. If he moved, the cop would break the arm he had twisted back around against the shoulder blade. Let's go, you bastard, let's go! And as they were pushing him up the steps Jeanne D'Arc spread her legs. With her fingertips she was holding her long crack open so Baptiste could drive it in hard. Next she would begin to scream and to scratch his back with her nails. Let's go, son of a bitch, let's go! Barthélémy closed his eyes. He couldn't struggle any more against the cops' violence. So, a night stick gouging him in the ribs, he went up the steps. He tripped in the doorway. The cops thought he was trying to get away again, so they gave him another beating, stopping only when they saw that Barthélémy was unconscious. They dragged him roughly down the hall and threw him into the old parents' bed. He was left in darkness but for the narrow strip of light directly in front of his eyes into which stepped Jeanne D'Arc as she came up from the basement. Fred held her around the waist, his eyes swaddling her in softness. The large breast was a star beneath the torn blouse. Ahhhhh! said Barthélémy before disappearing completely into the hippopotamus' maw where he dreamed a final, obscure dream, the very one which would force him to kill Jeanne D'Arc once and for all. So that he crawled for a long time still in the corridor of his shame, slithering like a serpent. Then he stuck his head through the basement window. He saw the patrol car pull up quickly in front of the old parents' house, he saw Fred push the door open, he saw Jeanne D'Arc toss her bags in the back and take a seat beside Fred, turning towards him; then the car came alive with a jolt and sped away. Barthélémy ran a hand through his hair. Something began to stir in his stomach, growing, rising, filling his entire being. That's how the final dream ended, at the very moment Barthélémy was setting the derby hat back on his head. Then he began to laugh: beneath his hat roared the furious waters of the river of evil forces; it would soon overflow into every corner of the house. And what could be better than laughter to signal evil's attack against Jeanne D'Arc? Through narrowed eyes he watched his sinuous laughter's steady progress across the surrounding darkness, watched it twine round the solid world, uproot it, send it crashing down. Everything would become slimy, foul with the stench of infection, fever-racked, and at the very heart of it all he would have to carry out the act which would liberate him. The derby was really a shiny silver helmet, and the saw — what could it be but the magic sword with which he would slay the fabled dragon, out of whose blood-smeared face shot the flames of sin? Thus he climbed the rickety steps, swallowing with difficulty, his ears ringing. All at once he saw the dragon's terrifying tail, the spiked feet clawing the linoleum, his thick tongue from behind which the small, cunning eyes were staring at him. He crossed himself and rushed the dragon. He didn't need to even think about what he was doing, he would be carried along by his movements, by his dancing feet, by the circular motion of the saw above his head. The dragon was rolling on the floor; his broken tail prevented him from pouncing and each kick to his body brought a bellow of impotence from him. His jaws were opening and closing like the nuns' and schoolmarms' wooden 'clacker' of old, calling no one now to order. Barthélémy leapt upon the dragon and crushed the beast's head beneath his heel. The dragon's huge feet curled up and the kitchen's beams split when he landed on his back. Barthélémy let out a terrifying scream and vomited up on the lifeless body all that was odious in him. (Then, frantically, he went to work.) First he spread Jeanne D'Arc's legs as far as they would go without breaking, then he cracked the bones in her hands and wrists, ripped off her kneecaps, reached and tore her pubic hair out. Then he squatted over Jeanne D'Arc's bust, trying to think of what more he should do before using the saw. All he could come up with was to fart several times on her tits. But the silver chain around her neck gave him another idea. He twisted it with his fingers as hard as he could. The head rose into the shadow, then he let it fall back to the floor. He did this over and over, listening to the dull sound, the watermelon-thump of the head striking the floor. When he grew tired of this game he went looking for a piece of wood. He found something better: a metal pipe. He returned to the kitchen, straddled Jeanne D'Arc's body, knees even with her tits, then put the metal pipe beneath the chain and began to twist. He was making a tourniquet which would keep all she was guilty of trapped in her head. He didn't stop till the white bone showed through the neck's lacerated flesh. Then he reached and took the saw and began to saw her limbs. His rage was such that soon in the middle of the kitchen there was only a trunk with blood squirting out of the stumps where the arms and legs had been. He couldn't seem to bring himself to cut off the head. Maybe he didn't have the right to do that; if he committed that act, everything would collapse, he wouldn't really have liberated himself: the falseness of his method would become obvious to him and he wouldn't find another that would be any more efficacious. It was better to wait, put off the event, since once her head was severed Jeanne D'Arc could never come back. (Why *should* it all unfold easily, why *should* the solution to the mysteries be found quickly?) But his hands finally touched the saw and

98

the blade made its way into the flesh, quickly reaching the bone and cutting through it. The head rolled onto the floor between Barthélémy's legs. He looked at the mass of bloody hair, thinking of nothing at all. Never had he been so distant from what was going through his own mind. Inside him and around him everything was becoming blurred, the furniture was losing its outlines, it had no depth, no contrast, it was merging into the white immensity of the room. The walls, the ceilings, how quickly it was all disappearing without artifice to hold it in place. And Barthélémy leaning over Jeanne D'Arc's severed head, and Barthélémy, and Barthélémy's crocodile tears! (A few insignificant actions remained, however, like dragging the trunk towards him. He was crying, he would have liked not to commit this next profanation with the contempt it showed; the idea was born of his trouble and pain. He stroked his prick with a bloody hand. When it was hard he opened the sticky lips and sank into the disfigured cunt. He was breathing heavily, terrified by the perversity of his act, his eyes closed so as not to see the awful cadaver. Nothing would remain of all this if not the movement of his prick going in and out, if not the full, depraved ejaculation. Had he killed Jeanne D'Arc just to commit this outrage on her?) And getting his pleasure this way, falling on the mutilated body and kissing the severed head, sent him tumbling head over heels into the void of his own death. And Barthélémy tore himself away from the evil and lunged backward, his bloody face twitching uncontrollably, his tongue stuck between his clenched teeth. The wind was opening and closing the kitchen door noisily, the curtains were billowing, the blind was a white tongue hanging in front of the window. He began to run wildly about the kitchen trying to escape; it felt as though the derby were screwed into his head, he had to get it off. He slammed into a wall with his shoulder, the derby went tock-tock as it hit the furniture; too many odors — of blood, of urine, of excrement — came into his nose. (Outside rain was falling once again. It sounded like heavy nails were hitting the tin roof, like rubber balls were bouncing off the windows. The big wet dog must have taken cover in his house, looking at the lightning through the crack between the two strips of burlap nailed over his door.) Barthélémy moved away from the window, squatted down and moved back to the middle of the kitchen, propelled by his hands. He reached and took the derby, which sat on Jeanne D'Arc's stomach. He put it back on his head before looking at the ragged limbs. They had already stopped bleeding. There was nothing more to be afraid of: everything threatening had flown out of the half-open window, been swallowed up in flames or fallen through the trap door leading to the nether regions of the cruel, vicious basement. He gathered the legs and the arms, the trunk and the head, reassembled them on the old carpet and lay down in front of them. He filled his pipe, lit it, burned his thumb trying to pack down the tobacco, swallowed the smoke which he then exhaled through his nose, reminding him of the dragon and the fire coming out of his large nostrils. He told himself he'd arrived, but where? Maybe killing Jeanne D'Arc wasn't enough, mutilating and committing outrage on her were surely no end nor a deliverance to be wished for. Things were more subtle than that, less easily identified, it didn't all have to do with Jeanne D'Arc nor with himself, for that matter, nor with Baptiste's big hand placed defiantly in the secret hollow. He thought now he'd been tricked: had they made him go through this whole routine just to be able to shove it down his throat? Destroy his pride? To make him feel guilty for actions which once would have been collective and thus the self-assigned tasks of a multitude chanting around a fire over which on a spit of shame Jeanne D'Arc was slowly roasting? He saw the long brown bodies, the noses deformed by pieces of wood and gold rings, the pierced, abnormally elongated ears, the tatooed skin, the large drooping tits, the pricks resting in leather cups. He saw the reassuring chants, the sacred homilies addressed to the appeased gods at the height of the celebration. (He saw the noise of waves breaking against the rocks, the cries of the large white birds, the beating of wings, the howls of lean wild dogs in the silent forest, their nostrils widened to the scent of burning flesh; and he had been the first warrior to put out his hand, demanding part of the rump as his portion, and he had swallowed much meat so that anger and strength should re-enter his mind and body. After that he had been able to run all night through the forest. After that the only sound heard was the hiss of the white lances thrown against the shadows as they were chased to the other country there beyond the Outaouais where life became a hostile force.) Barthélémy's pipe went out. He stood up and ground the ashes beneath his bare foot. The night was sufficient unto itself now that the murder had been carried out and the patrol cars were buzzing like flies around devastated Morial Mort. Barthélémy opened the door and whistled for the dog to come out of his house. Standing on his hind legs, he began to bark. Barthélémy returned to the house, took Jeanne D'Arc's two legs, reopened the door with his foot and went down the steps. He advanced towards the dog, speaking to him so he would remain calm. Quiet, dog, quiet. (The heavy lance halved the air and sank into the wood of the dog house. The big dog saw the flesh, jumped on it and began to devour the thigh.) Munch a bunch of fritos, chimed Barthélémy, then went back inside the house where all that was left on the old carpet was Jeanne D'Arc's head. That Barthélémy couldn't give the big dog: the head had to be thrown into the basement where it would purify the evil forces. Thus he grabbed it by the hair, crossed the kitchen in a couple of hops and lifted the latch, then threw the head down the steps. Bonk, bonk, bonk. The night suddenly sank to the bottom of its own darkness. Barthélémy put his ear to the floor and listened. What he heard reassured him. The demons were already fighting over the head and rats were coming out to eat what was left. Once he'd washed the floor with Javel water he could at last change clothes, take the old man's harmonica out of its small velvet-lined case, unleash the dog and walk through Morial Mort towards the helicopters full of soldiers circling above Monselet Street)) –

((Terrebonne
February 1970 – November 1971))

Other Works by Victor-Lévy Beaulieu

NOVELS

La Nuitte de Malcomm Hudd
Oh Miami, Miami, Miami
Race du monde
Jos Connaissant

THEATRE

En attendant Trudot
Monsieur Zéro
Cérémonial pour l'assassinat d'un ministre
Ma Corriveau
La Tête de Monsieur Ferron

ESSAYS AND CRITICISM

Pour saluer Victor Hugo
Manuel de la petite littérature du Québec
Monsieur Melville (3 volumes)

IN TRANSLATION

The Grandfathers (translated by Marc Plourde)
Jack Kerouac: a Chicken-Essay
    (translated by Sheila Fischman)
Don Quixote in Nighttown (translated by Sheila Fischman)